Going Going Gondola

An Atticus Drake Mystery: Book 1

Tora Barry

Published in 2015 by Castleforge Books Ltd.

ISBN: 978-0-9932939-0-0

PROLOGUE

The taxi chugged across the water and the City grew larger and more beautiful. Passing through the islands in the lagoon, Atticus tried to imagine what travellers from many centuries ago would have felt, on seeing the same sights. It was familiar in one way, the stuff of chocolate boxes, postcards, a thousand photographs, and yet in reality it was very, marvellously, different. Close up, Venice was a stranger, a ghostly figure in a faded dress, irresistible, beckoning like a siren. If she had been leading him to his death he would not have been able to do anything but follow, and as the little boat with its reassuringly polished teak decks got closer, and eventually turned into the Grand Canal, deep in the heart of the City, Atticus shivered, though he was not cold.

Venice was indescribably beautiful, but somehow, it was not entirely benign.

Chapter One

Atticus Drake, five foot nine, almost forty, once dark hair now *un*fairly greying at the temples, but otherwise in reasonable shape, looked surreptitiously at his reflection in the huge mirror across the room. He had never been inside the Dorchester before, although he had loitered outside in Park Lane on many occasions, walking to or from a bus stop, or the Tube at Marble Arch, distracted from the seething traffic or the inviting green of Hyde Park by a horde of photographers waiting for an A-List celebrity, or the sweep of a limousine with blacked-out windows. The Dorchester, rather like London itself, he had always felt, was for other people. People who had money to throw about and other people to be seen with.

But now, here he was, not only inside the gleaming brass-adorned doors, not only well past the marbled hall, the long, richly-carpeted drawing room where business meetings were held and ladies lunched, but in the world-famous restaurant. Sitting on one side of a vast expanse of white tablecloth, in the company of an extremely beautiful blonde.

Around him people talked in quiet voices, their cutlery chinking peacefully against the china, glasses dancing with lead crystal and valuable wine. Waiters and sommeliers glided about as if on invisible castors, appearing at the elbows of the diners without warning, whisking away a plate, replacing a starched napkin and vanishing again so quickly that one scarcely believed they had been there at all. They clearly didn't expect any acknowledgment, which was a source of great relief to Atticus, who, somewhere between his A levels and his frankly lucky, time at Cambridge, had once been a waiter for a season in another London hotel and had lived in fear of being recognised by a fellow servant ever since. At which point he would of course be denounced as a fraud, forced to give up any pretence of being a diner in such an elegant establishment, and banished to the kitchen to continue washing up in a waistcoat.

In front of him was a perfectly balanced flute of champagne, tall, cool, and inviting, tiny bubbles rising to its surface like silly girls running towards the dance floor at a party. And across the table, with an amused look on her face, was Laura Hutchinson, the girl who had made his life in the Sixth Form at St Joseph's Community College such utter, utter hell.

"I *know* Darling!" she was saying, her voice musical, with that enticing hint of laughter in it. "I can hardly believe it myself. Almost fifteen years! Although I would never admit that to anyone else. I can't possibly be *thirty five* can I?"

It had been twenty years, almost to the day, and Atticus had counted the days. And he had been in the year below Laura at St Joseph's. And he was within a sniff of forty. "Surely not," he said politely.

"Those were the days, weren't they?" Laura said, swishing her long shiny hair about like a horse in a field, aware that the eyes of the room were on her.

"We had such a lot of fun. We were so cool back then, weren't we?"

Atticus took a long sip of his champagne not trusting himself to speak. He didn't believe he had ever been cool. Bryan Ferry was cool. David Bowie was cool. Atticus Drake was *nice*. Well brought up. A classic dresser without much interest in clothes, a useful sportsman if you were looking to make up a team, but never a goal scorer. A fan of a good book, a decent claret, a walk in the countryside on a cold day. A chap who fitted in anywhere but never really belonged.

"You were so - so -" Laura seemed to be searching for a word. He hoped it wasn't any of the words he was thinking of.

"Romantic!" she finished with a flourish. "Yes, that's it. I thought you were so Romantic."

That wasn't one of the words he had been thinking of. "*Romantic*?" he said, surprised.

"Like Simon Le Bon. Or George Michael. Or Byron."

Only Laura could put those three in a single bracket.

"I was a little bit in love with you, you know," she said.

Now that *was* a surprise. All Atticus knew was that way back then, for some three years and about three months, and maybe a couple of weeks, one of them had been in love and it hadn't been Laura.

Laura Hutchinson had sent notes asking him to meet her in unlikely places and then sent half a dozen of her giggling friends to laugh at him. Laura Hutchinson had stolen his underpants when the class went swimming and attached them to the flagpole at the school's gates. Laura Hutchinson had told her *boyfriend*, Vince Peacock, that Atticus had made a pass at her in the library and Vince Peacock had locked him in the bogs overnight to teach him a lesson. Laura Hutchinson had written a poem in class about a hopeless loser who killed himself because he was in love with a beautiful girl who didn't even know he existed and called her poem *Atticus Drake*.

And it had been all the more terrible because no matter what she did, or how hard he tried to get over it, he had been completely, massively, and hopelessly in love with her. He had thought about her, day and night. He had imagined her, in a wedding dress, sailing up the aisle of the local church, framed by flowers, to meet him, her future husband. He had dreamt about the two of them, running through fields in the rain, or standing in meadows of wild flowers. In Assembly, he imagined her lovely silky hair slipping through his hands, and how it would feel to touch the beautiful toned brown skin of her legs where they met the hem of her illegally short school skirt.

And then, in a rush of burnt school books and flour bombing and empty promises, term and school were over, and she had gone, and Atticus was alone. Laura Hutchinson had been Atticus's first, totally unrequited, love.

Laura Hutchinson who had now tracked him down through St Joseph's proud list of Oxbridge alumni, and found his number, and asked him to go to lunch with her, in London, at the Dorchester. "My treat," she had said, and now she was sitting across a table from him in a tiny bright pink linen shift dress. Several considerable jewels hung about her like decorations on an interior designer's Christmas tree, and her long, long legs wound elegantly round each other before ending in the most marvellous pink suede sandals with heels that must have been six inches high. He was glad she had been sitting down when he arrived. He wondered vaguely how he would manage to get out of the Dorchester without standing up himself, and demonstrating how far short of Laura he fell in inches, never mind loveliness.

And now she was telling him she thought of him as *Byron*. The vision of his *Wacky Races* underpants, fluttering in the breeze above the Headmaster's head on School Open Day came hurtling back, and he felt his face go red.

"You're embarrassed," said Laura, reaching across the table and putting a beautifully manicured hand on his arm. "Oops. Didn't you *know*? I had *such* a crush on you!"

The starters arrived, tiny morsels of fish on vast plates, sprinkled with wild flowers and dotted about with green and yellow blobs of jelly. Atticus wondered how it would be possible to eat a mouthful of it, without accidentally eating all of it at once.

"*Gorge,*" pronounced Laura, who had somehow managed it. He sat transfixed, as her lovely lips moved in ecstasy, her eyes closed, long lashes sweeping her cheeks. He sucked on a small nasturtium-like leaf. He imagined having sex with Laura, wild, sudden, passionate sex, probably standing up. In the coat cupboard right here in the foyer of this hotel, amongst furs and suede and cashmere jackets. What would Lord Byron do? Come to think of it, what would Simon Le Bon do?

"So Darling," she was saying, "What do you do with yourself these days? Are you *really* important?"

Atticus's days, all the ones before this one, stretched out behind him, a vast empty road with no redeeming features, no landmarks, no battle scars, not even a milestone to mark some kind of achievement. Then, as if operating a 360 degree scroll on the Google Earth App, he swung round to look at all the tomorrows. And there was nothing there either.

"Oh, you know," he said, "This and that. I did some Land Management after Cambridge. Then I spent some time helping a mate run a hotel in Scotland. After that I went into the City. Money markets. All a long time ago obviously."

"How *clever!*" said Laura, looking interested, "And did you make *mountains* of lovely dosh?"

"Well a bit." said Atticus.

"*Darling,*" said Laura, putting her hand over his and with a deeply sympathetic look on her lovely face, and looking him up and down, taking in his well-worn jacket and trousers. "And did you lose it *all*?"

"Well, actually...." Atticus said, "I didn't really have time to. One day I was at my desk, the next I was standing on the pavement holding a cardboard box with a spider plant in it. Nobody really discussed what was happening. Technically I was lucky. Luckier than the ones who stayed."

"Poor you," said Laura, "It must have been *vile*."

Her words, pronounced so carefully, so soothingly, had an extraordinary effect on Atticus. He suddenly felt completely, *actually* devastated.

"And now?" Laura seemed to be hanging on his every word. Waiters took away plates and Atticus realised that in the end he hadn't even eaten the fish. It was hardly going to make the difference between nutrition and starvation. Bigger plates loomed, like flying saucers, and landed in front of them. Laura nodded approvingly at the waiter who melted into a soft pulp in gratitude, as though the sun had been turned on him and he was made of chocolate.

"Well now, I suppose, I just do a bit of this and that," he said, lamely, knowing he did neither this nor that. "I'm learning to play the cello," he finished.

"How *fab*," purred Laura. "How *clever*."

"I'm not very good." said Atticus.

"I bet you are," Laura said smoothly, "I bet you're bloody brilliant." She beckoned to a waiter who brought new glasses, and poured wine.

"It's Merseault," Laura whispered. "I love Merseault, don't you?"

Atticus did love Merseault. But it was a long time since he had had any. Somehow it didn't seem right, drinking fine wine on your own. And they didn't serve it at the Rifleman's Arms, the faux-spit-and-sawdust pub on the corner of the new Docklands road in which he lived. The champagne had already started to go to his head, together with the atmosphere and the sheer unbelievable quality of the position he was in.

"Well, I think classical music's terribly important," he said boldly.

"Of *course* it is," said Laura.

Did she believe that? Atticus seemed to remember Laura being more of a disco and Ibiza girl. He found he was imagining sex again. This time on a beach, rolling surf crashing round them, Laura's incredible body wound round his own, which had somehow acquired rather more muscle and tone than it had boasted that morning.

Back at the Dorchester, his shirt was sticking to his back under the linen of his jacket. The main course had been delivered, almost without him noticing. He looked down at the plate, the tiny square of lamb glistening pinkly as it lay back on its green bed of wilted spinach, trailing its sinewy fingers lazily in the little stream of gravy which flowed past. A little hedgerow of what had been described as 'foraged vegetables' framed the scene. It was positively pastoral.

"So Laura," he said bravely. "What is it exactly, that *you* do these days? You look very, well...*well*."

If it had been possible to kick himself under the table he would have done it. Laura was laughing.

Oh, that laugh. Beautiful, and very slightly, even now, mocking. How was a man to differentiate between the two? Was it worth enduring the mockery to hear it? Having heard it again, could he imagine life without it?

"Do? well I don't really *do* anything. I don't really need to. I'm *desperately* idle. Although I suppose what I *actually* do, is arrange things."

"Arrange things? Flowers? Antiques?"

"People."

"People?"

"I arrange people. You think people meet each other, do business deals, fall in love, run countries, by accident? Of course they don't. They need to be advised, moved around, *introduced*."

"The right place at the right time, sort of thing?"

"Exactly. You see, I *knew* you were clever. You understand me perfectly." Laura sighed sadly. "So few people truly get me, you know Atticus? Oh I'm successful, rich, popular, of course I am. But sometimes, I just wish I was, oh well, you don't want to hear all that do you?

I do, I do, I do, I do, I *do!* sang Atticus in his heart. What he actually said was,

"So do you, are you... you must ...have, well, someone? A husband perhaps?"

"A husband?" exclaimed Laura as if Atticus had suggested she had a rat in her handbag, "Good Lord no. I did have a husband once, and don't get me wrong, he was *very* good to me." She fingered the pear shaped pink diamond she was wearing on a fine chain round her neck, "But in the end, I just thought, Laura,you are too young and too full of life to be kept in a cage, even a golden one. You understand?"

"Oh of course," said Atticus, swiftly replacing the Laura of the village church and the wedding dress in his dream with a vision of the two of them speeding across a Mediterranean bay in a fast boat, hair flying behind, joy and freedom on their faces, love in their hearts, and the sun in their eyes.

"You," said Laura, breaking into his daydream, "Is there a little wife in your life?"

Atticus suddenly thought of Flora, cheerful, unspoilt, pretty like a rose in a country garden. He felt suddenly guilty, but Flora just wouldn't go into that imaginary speedboat, no matter how hard he tried to put her there.

"No. No-one." he said.

"Ah," said Laura, touching his arm again and sending an electric shock into the back of his head. "Do you know, I suspect you're not telling me the whole truth? But I shall let you get away with it, my lovely Lord Byron, because you are wicked and wonderful, and I suggest you have broken a whole string of hearts."

Atticus wondered for a moment when Laura had developed this poetic streak, and in fact, now he came to think of it, where she had got any idea of who Byron was. As far as he remembered, she had spent most English lessons either playing truant in the bus shelters at the bottom of the town, or, if forced to attend, drawing Vince Peacock's name and assorted intertwined love hearts, on pencilcases, desks and herself, with coloured felt pens.

Another waiter hovered delicately, waiting for a break in Laura's flow of floral language to clear the plates away. He looked up and with a shock realised he was staring into the face of one of the crew from the Bloomsbury Hilton, circa 1995. Geoff. Jim, Jules, something like that. Geoff-Jim-Jules winked as he leant forward to place the huge dessert menus in front of them. "*Pudding* sir," he said menacingly, into Atticus's ear.

Laura made a small excusing gesture and got up. "Don't go away Darling, I'll be right back," she said, and left the table. As she crossed the room, it was as though she was drawing a long thread behind her, on which were hooked the hopes and dreams of every man in the room. Atticus could still smell her perfume, as the lights went out in his heart.

What did she want? Why had she asked him here, after all this time? He so wanted to believe she really wanted him, that she had, as she assured him, really missed him. He tried to tell himself, he was a grown up now, someone with his own life, plenty to offer. But however he tried, he couldn't really believe it. Laura Hutchinson had always been out of his league. Now with her diamonds and her Mulberry handbag and her Dorchester, she was surely out of his reach.

But then again, he was the one sitting in the striped dining chair with the huge fabric bow on it, the one with the remaining half glass of an extremely good 1996 *Les Charmes* Merseault in front of him, and Geoff or Jim or whatever his name was, was the one now carrying a small dog out of the restaurant ahead of an imperious matron with a walking frame.

Atticus Drake was the man with the staggeringly beautiful girl at his table.

There was an audible gasp and he realised Laura was on her way back. He thought at one point there might actually be a round of applause. She sank elegantly into her chair, and leant across to him. "Did you miss me?" she whispered.

"Like the devil," he said.

She laughed, which was not the reaction he had been hoping for. "You *are* sweet," she said, which was even worse. God, this was almost more torture than the school stuff had been.

"Souffle," she said vaguely over her shoulder and in an instant the menus had disappeared again, and a flurry of spoons and plates and new napkins ensued. Atticus, who had been wondering whether to go for the melee of summer fruits or the frozen mocha parfait and weighing up which one was likely to be bigger, fought a small wave of disappointment.

"So Atticus," said Laura taking his head in her hands and turning his face so he was looking deep into her pale blue eyes. "I have just had a wonderful idea."

Was it too much to hope she had seen the coat cupboard too?

"Now that I have found you again, I don't intend to let you go."

"Fine by me," said a small slightly whiny voice from somewhere inside Atticus.

"And it just so happens....."

Geoff-Jim-Jules chose that precise moment to make his point. Forcibly separating them, he leant in between them, and placed a large fluffy, apricot-scented cloud of sugar on the table.

"Souffle," he said, menacingly, "Don't leave it a moment longer, it's perfect."

It had been. Almost. But now there was the souffle to contend with. And although it was utterly delicious, quite incredibly light and yet full of fruit, and even though sharing it meant their spoons were constantly touching, Atticus felt as though he could kill.

And although he waited, dropping gentle hints, until the last airy teaspoonful had disappeared into that perfect mouth, and the dish was cleared, and replaced by tiny expresso coffees in bone china thimbles, accompanied by exquisite chocolates and striped candy, and brandy balloons in which a scarce millimetre of cognac shifted thickly and threatened him with an afternoon headache, Laura didn't mention her marvellous idea again.

They had stretched out the coffee and brandy as far as it would go. Around them the room had emptied, the waiting staff now faded into the background, merging into the regency striped wallpaper, yet Atticus still felt watched. And exhausted. What had been the point? His world had been turned upside down, he had been reminded of things it had taken two decades for him to forget, and for what?

Laura was looking at him fondly. "Penny for them," she said.

Panicking, Atticus tried to think of something witty and interesting to say. Failing that, something which might remind her that she was about to suggest taking him upstairs to a fabulous suite and making love to him until the sun went down.

"Vince," he said without realising it. "What happened to Vince?"

"Vince?" said Laura, "Vince who?"

Atticus could hear a small but distinctive buzzing sound. Looking down at the small upholstered stool between them which had been provided for Laura's handbag, he realised it was moving.

"Sorry Darling," she said, "It's on silent, but you know how it is."

Reaching a long hand into the silky depths of the buttersoft Mulberry Classic, she pulled out a small white mobile phone. She look surreptitiously round with a wicked grin, and for a moment, Atticus saw the Laura Hutchinson of St Joseph's, the truant with the cigarettes in her bumbag, and the lipstick concealed in her bra. She looked intently at the screen for a moment, frowned and then laughed. Then she replaced the phone in her handbag. Then she said the words he realised he had been dreading since she arrived at the table, which seemed like a lifetime ago.

"Darling, I must go. Business to see to, you understand."

"People to arrange?" said Atticus, slightly peevishly. He knew he was in danger of behaving like a spoilt child. After all he had just had what was probably the most expensive lunch of his life, with the most beautiful woman in the world. Had he imagined that it was going to last for ever? That they would grow old together, flirting and imagining wild sex in exotic locations until they were both in their nineties (Laura no doubt still insisting she wasn't a day over fifty)?

"Indeed," said Laura, getting up. Immediately several waiters reappeared from the misty corners of the room to assist. None of them made any attempt to help Atticus, who struggled out from behind the table and tried to smooth the creases out of his jacket before anybody noticed it looked as though he had slept in it.

The made their way out of the restaurant, and were halfway down the long carpeted hall before Atticus realised nobody had presented, or paid the bill. The staff were ritually nodding their heads respectfully, brandishing pashminas and offering umbrellas, leaping to open doors ahead of Laura, as Atticus trailed scruffily in her wake.

As they reached the steps and the noise and the dirt of Park Lane came towards them, Laura turned to Atticus and put a hand on his arm.

"Here's my idea," she said at last. "There's a party. It's tomorrow night. Not far, just round the corner from here. Some friends of mine. You must come. You will come, won't you? *Please*?"

She thrust a small white card in his hand,which he failed to register, as he looked into her lovely face, with its clear, pleading blue eyes. She sounded as though she really wanted him to be at that party.

"I should be delighted," he said.

Then Laura Hutchinson, goddess of the sixth form, leant slightly forward and kissed him. Absolutely and thoroughly, on the mouth. Coming up for air, Atticus could no longer see Park Lane nor feel the dust in the air. The Dorchester had disappeared, and all he was left with was a heavenly cloud of excitement, and lust, and pink linen, and glossy blonde hair, and the promise of a future.

There was a noise behind him and he turned to see the doorman, handing him his own, tatty telescopic umbrella, which had come apart from its cover and looked like a handful of dead crow.

Turning back, Laura had gone.

Chapter Two

It was ironic really. Throughout his short career in the City, one of Atticus's biggest problems had been lack of sleep. He, like most of his colleagues, had been more or less permanently tired. They would leave the office, brains still working overtime, and head for the nearest pub or wine bar to wind down. Then, the first drinks would fuel the next, and the next, and if food was to be eaten it would invariably be not very much and late at night, so that by the time he got back to his Docklands apartment, there was barely enough time to undress, lie down and close his eyes before having to get up again, shower and find a clean shirt before grabbing oily double-strength coffee on the run and heading back to the office.

When it all came to an end, and after the initial phase of complete disorientation had been followed by a spell of euphoria at being free, then by a wave of depression at being unwanted in a job he had got used to, and as he was apparently completely unsuited to anything else, he had hoped he would find sleep easier. His doctor had advised him to avoid stress, coffee, alcohol, too much television, too much reading, too much of anything really, and instead to redesign his life, with plenty of good food and fresh air.

And yet, ever since the day they had turfed him unceremoniously out of the office, bewildered and with the eyes of his former colleagues upon him, that curious mixture of sympathy and relief piercing the back of his head, he hadn't really been able to sleep at all.

Night after night, he lay awake in his huge bed, spread himself diagonally across the middle of the vast white cotton space, arms outstretched, and tried and tried to sleep, but all that came were brief bursts of unconsciousness, filled with wild dreams and imaginings so muddled that when he woke up he was more exhausted than ever.

He had thought that taking up the cello might help, that concentrating on something new might wear his brain out a bit, but after each of his lessons with the terrifying Miss Millard he dreamed of feral orchestras terrorising cities, and wild animals swaying in time to the Elgar *Cello Concerto*.

He asked his sister Hilly for advice and tried aromatherapy oils, but woke with the worst headache he had ever experienced and smelled of sandalwood and patchouli for days, attracting quite the wrong sort of attention on the bus. He had tried relaxation tapes which left him, wide awake as the soothing voice faded out, worrying about whether he would die prematurely from a heart attack, or whether the smoke alarms in the building had been checked thoroughly, or if he had forgotten somebody's birthday.

Some hours after he had returned from The Dorchester, having paced a thousand times across the floor of his open-plan sitting-dining-kitchen-come-small-ballroom, he phoned Hilly.

As he waited for her to answer it, he imagined it, sitting on a table in Hilly's big untidy house in Cambridge, surrounded by children's toys and half-eaten apples, and piles of books and newspapers and evidence of real family life. The scene was in stark contrast to his own apartment, with its sleek white lines and bachelor-pad accessories. As he wandered round the room, the phone held to his ear, he rifled through his own pile of unread newspapers to make the place look untidier.

"It's nearly midnight!" a muffled voice, thick with deep-set weariness protested.

"Sorry. Were you asleep?"

"As I said, it's nearly midnight. Of course I'm not asleep."

"Can't you hear?" Hilly was holding the phone at arms length. In the background, Atticus could make out a rising crescendo of wailing as the one or both of the twins cottoned on to the fact that their mother's attention was not focussed solely on them.

"Ah," he said. "Perhaps this isn't a good time after all."

"Your bloody nieces have had a total of twenty minutes sleep each, not simultaneously of course, that would be far too easy, and during the remaining twenty three hours and forty minutes of today have wrecked the playroom, spread cereal and beans all over the kitchen, broken the knobs off the washing machine, and spilt cranberry juice over Hal's dress shirt, just as I had finished ironing it because he has to go to a works dinner tomorrow, and now he's online trying to order another one which probably won't come in time, so, yes, it's a great time for you to call. In that no time is a great time, unless you're calling to tell me you're going to drive up here right now and take them away to live with you. For ever."

"Sorry," said Atticus. "I can't sleep either. Just phoned for a chat really."

"It's probably the genes," said Hilly gloomily. "I shall hold you responsible for ever for the fact that your nieces have inherited rampant insomnia. Anyway, I'm here now. Chat away."

"I've been invited to a cocktail party."

"Have you? Lucky old you. I'll put *Hello* magazine on standby."

"Perhaps I'd better start at the beginning. I had lunch today at The Dorchester"

"Hold the front page. No kidding? You?"

"You don't need to sound quite so surprised. I do get asked out occasionally."

"I know. You're lovely. The ideal date. Don't mind me. I've just lost my sense of human."

"You mean humour."

"I know what I mean. Of course I'm thrilled for you. Especially after, well you know, after Flora. I'm glad you're getting out and about again. But The *Dorchester?* Was it utterly swank City?"

"It was," admitted Atticus. "I went with Laura Hutchinson."

"Who?"

"Laura Hutchinson. You remember her, year above me at St Joe's."

"No, no. I can't remember her. What does she look like?"

Atticus was overwhelmed by a vision of Laura, resplendent in a hot pink minidress, impossibly high heels running towards him, arms outstretched, hair swinging in the breeze.

"Gorgeous. Tall, slim, leggy, blonde, unspeakably glamourous."

"I hate her. But I still can't remember her. However, my memory is made of mashed banana. Unless Laura Hutchinson is a new organic pea and kale pasta sauce she just won't register I'm afraid."

"Well anyway, she called me. Out of the blue. Got my number from Peterhouse."

"And you haven't seen her since school? And she took you to The *Dorchester*?"

"I wish you wouldn't keep saying it like that. I am fairly presentable you know."

"I know. Sorry. I just can't imagine it somehow."

"Me lunching at the Dorchester?"

"The outside world."

"Poor bunny, They won't always be four you know."

"I know. At least I try to believe it. And then sometimes, when they're all quiet, asleep in the pyjamas, or playing in the garden so only the neighbours can hear them scream, I know I'll miss the three-year-old them very much when they're all grown up and too embarrassed to be seen with me, and they're the ones having lunch at The Dorchester."

"*I'll* take you to the Dorchester then. And we can spy on them from a corner table."

"I might just hold you to that. If I'm not too feeble to walk by then. Anyway, back to you. What prompted this sudden resurgence of interest in my little brother?"

"I know. It does sound odd. And now she's invited me to a cocktail party. In someone's house. In Mayfair."

There was a huge crash in the background and the ominous silence which always precedes an almighty three-year-old shriek.

"Darling I think I will probably have to go and deal with that one. Hal's already fully deployed dealing with the coal bucket incident from earlier. Call me again, let me know how you get on?"

"You think I should go then? To the cocktail party in Mayfair?"

"Hell yes. I've always wondered what those houses are like inside. You might meet someone who can offer you a job. At any rate, you can have another eyeful of the lovely Lara."

"Laura."

"Yes, Laura. Still don't remember her. Although...."

There was another crash and the phone went dead.

Atticus rifled through his collection of four clean shirts several times during the following day, trying to decide which one to wear. What did people wear to cocktail parties? What exactly *was* a cocktail party?

In the end he decided on an old favourite, a black suit, which had been so well worn that the jacket was more like a cardigan. That way if he was overdressed he could pretend it *was* a cardigan, whip the tie off and put his hands in the jacket pockets, transforming himself immediately from smart party guest back to bumbling creative-academic type.

He emerged from the Tube at Tower Hill in the early evening, and decided to take a cab from there.

"Nice," said the cab driver as he turned into the wide Mayfair street the name of which Atticus had read scrawled on the back of Laura's business card . "I thought these were all embassies and Black Russians."

"Perhaps they are," Atticus said, getting out some house numbers short of his target, so he could collect his thoughts on the short walk to the door.

Back in Cambridge, Hilly came in from the long garden with yet another basket of washing and dropped it in the middle of the kitchen floor.

"Hal? Hal!" she shouted.

Hal came running downstairs two at a time. Seeing his wife still upright, and seemingly unkilled by an intruder, he stopped, confused.

"What?" he said. "I was right in the middle of the a project report! I thought you were being abducted by white slavers! Whatever is the matter?"

"I've just remembered who Laura Hutchinson is," said Hilly.

Chapter Three

Atticus stood outside the building looking up at the glossy black door. It was an elegant town house, double fronted, several storeys high, with bay windows, all of which seemed to have been blacked out, as if the house couldn't bear to look at the other side of the street. The house immediately opposite was exactly the same, it was as though he was standing between two maiden aunts who had once had a row over a stuffed olive and hadn't spoken since.

He shifted from foot to foot, wondering if he should ring a bell, or if the door would just open if he leant on it. It didn't look inviting. Atticus was used to the sort of party where the door stood wide open and early arrivals were already lying across the doorstep, or where a hugely efficient wife brandished a tray of canapés, greeting guests with a list of the credentials of the other guests. 'Oh Atticus, you simply must meet Sophie, she's in Futures, and there's Tony, he's something terribly important at the Arts Council, Tony, this is Atticus, he *used to be* something terribly impressive in the City.'

Atticus often wondered how long it would be before someone would introduce him as something he was, or was going to be, rather than something he *once* was.

He heard a scuffle and a giggle, and saw a tall man with a very black handlebar moustache, in an almost full-length overcoat coming up the street with a scantily-clad six-foot woman on each arm. Standing aside to let them pass, he watched as they negotiated the steps with difficulty on stork-like legs in very high heels, the man propped between them. As the door opened, he decided on a whim to slip in behind them.

Unsure as to whether this would be the kind of party where you were expected to bring a bottle, Atticus had done so, and the heavy weight of the *Veuve Clicquot* had pulled his jacket out of shape on one side. After a quick glance at the trio entering the house, he made a late decision to jettison the bottle, and stowed it neatly behind a rhododendron at the top of the steps to the basement of the building. He could always claim he had left it in the car, if it proved to be necessary.

Thus relieved of his glass burden, his jacket dropping decorously off one shoulder and enveloped in a cloud of *Dior* and *Poison*, with a hint of Cuban cigar, wafting over the shoulders of the trio ahead, he was swept into the hall of the house and the door closed surprisingly silently behind him.

At this point he had expected to find himself in a large space, and stepped confidently forward, only to find his mouth full of hair extensions. The women in front of him hadn't moved on, for the simple reason that there was another door in front of them, and all four were now standing in a space the size of a small lift.

The man in the long coat spoke in a low voice, saying something Atticus couldn't quite catch, and the girls laughed shrilly and tossed their hair about like pedigree borzoi. Atticus bent his knees to avoid whiplash.

Just as he thought he might suffocate, the door in front of them opened and the hall materialised. There was a flurry of coats, and some more giggling as a pair of imposing doormen inspected something given to them by the man in front of him.

With a start, Atticus realised it was some sort of invitation. The doorman read the document carefully, looking up from time to time as if to verify its provider, before stepping neatly aside to let them pass.

The thick clouds of scent dissipated, and Atticus was left exposed, knees still slightly bent, looking up into the faces of the doormen. The problem with the invitation thing was that he didn't have one.

He stood up hastily, raising himself to his full two-thirds-of-doorman height, and patted his pockets apologetically. Everybody waited.

"Look," he said eventually, his voice echoing off the walls, ricocheting off the marble of the staircase and coming back to hit him in the face. "The thing is, I was asked to come here. By a friend. I mean, I was invited. Properly. Well not properly as it happens, or I'd have a written invitation. But still.....

"I mean how would I know the address if I hadn't been invited? I'm hardly the sort of man who cruises the neighbourhood looking for a party. Well, not this kind of neighbourhood anyway. And anyway I haven't actually done that since I was a student. Except for New Years' Eve 1999, obviously. But that was a party just looking for us really...

"My friend, the one who invited me. Is she here do you think? Tall, blonde, beautiful. Well you'd hardly say if she was or she wasn't would you? I mean those two, those two who have just gone in, they're quite nice looking girls too, aren't they? But it would be rude to comment. My friend, Laura, that's it - Laura! Her name is Laura. Anyway, I met her yesterday and she asked me to come to this, er..party..."

Silence.

"There *is* a party here, isn't there?...."

Some time later, as he sat on the steps outside the house, and before the level of the *Veuve Clicqot* fell below the half way point, Atticus suddenly had a thought. A few moments later, warm with the confidence only Champagne drunk very fast on an empty stomach can bring, and brandishing Laura's business card, Atticus presented himself once again to the doormen.

"I think you'll find I have an appointment," he said firmly.

And to his slight surprise, the doormen stood back, and waved him in.

Atticus looked round the cavernous hall, as he walked across the black and white tiled floor being careful not to step on the lines. Around him were several closed doors, and there seemed little option but to start up the huge staircase which dominated the hall. His soft-soled shoes squeaked on the marble.

"Not suede darling!" he heard his mother say in a horrified voice in his head, "Only a cad wears suede shoes."

"Cads and Elvis," Hilly had pointed out once.

"Rather the same thing I should think," their mother had said.

There was a succession of huge oil paintings on the wall as he ascended, vast severe faces of military chaps with swords and horses and whole receding counties behind them. It must be odd, he thought, to be commissioned to paint someone bigger than they really are. The real person must look so insignificant when you finally stop work and go out for a drink or whatever.

He suspected a couple of the paintings of being extremely serious artworks. Atticus was hardly an expert but his mother, had brought them up in a world of colour and oil paint and enthusiasm for art, and in his financial heyday, he had seen a few great pieces change hands amongst clients. He ran his hand across a large white piece of marble on a plinth on the landing before realising he had inadvertently felt up a reclining nude.

"Sorry," he said without thinking, his voice echoing.

He heard a noise, faint, muffled by miles of thick walls and reinforced doors, but vaguely, party-like. He headed on up a second flight of stairs and found a handful of extremely well dressed men standing in a huddle.

They turned and looked at him.

"Am I in the right place?" he said, more cheerfully than he felt. "The Worzel Gummidge Fancy Dress Party in Aid of the Sartorially Challenged?"

One of the men nodded at a door opposite. Nobody spoke.

"Well I can't stand around chatting to you all day," Atticus said, "I need a drink." And he took the deep breath of a man about to perform a cliff dive in an unreliable pair of Speedos and opened the door.

Luckily, he had found the party. The room was full of people standing about in groups, while waiters in tailcoats circulated with trays of large drinks, and plates of very small food. Atticus ate a choux pastry swan, a striped fish made of cheese, and a prawn which he realised slightly too late was wrapped round a skewer. Then he accepted a tumbler of what looked like paraffin but which tasted like whisky and, as it happened, was extremely effective in taking away the pain caused by the skewer.

He decided to circulate. As he cruised gently round the room, he caught snatches of conversation, above the music, which was being provided by a severe-faced string quartet. He was reminded of his music teacher, Miss Millard. Looking at their faces he decided that these were her relatives. He hoped he wouldn't get so drunk he would offer to have a go on the cello.

He drifted round the edge of the room for a while, like a skater hanging onto the side of the rink, grinning hopefully at people who responded by turning away. Then almost as soon as he had arrived, he found himself out of the room again, as a smaller door at the back of the room opened, to let a waiter with an empty tray through. Swept along, Atticus realised he was on another small landing, where three large men were loading something into a service lift. They didn't notice him, and continued to bundle their cargo, a large heavy item wrapped in tarpaulin, into the small space, grunting and puffing as they did so.

"You said you'd get it sorted," one swore under his breath.

"And I will, I *will*. Keep yer hair on," said another, "Ere. You got the other end?"

"I've got it," puffed the third, "You never said it would be this heavy."

"Yeah well, you never know till the job's done do yer? Anyway, nobody's the same size lying down as they are standing up are they?"

"You should know. I've seen your missus. She's definitely taller lying down."

The three laughed, and slammed the gate across the lift before hitting the button. The lift cranked into life and the ominous bundle descended out of sight.

Then the men turned and saw Atticus.

Nobody said anything. For a very long time.

"Evening," said Atticus eventually in a very high voice. "I was er, looking for...."

"Yeah?" said one of the men, coming up very close to Atticus and breathing sweaty cigarette and hot-dog breath in his face. "Well whatever it is you're looking for, it's not here right?"

"Um, well, evidently," said Atticus backing away, only to find he was up against a wall. He looked round for a way of escape, but the door he had come through was now closed and a very long way away.

"And now you're in the wrong place," the man continued, "What we've all got to decide now, is if it's the wrong time." If this was a TV drama, Atticus decided, he'd cast Ray Winstone.

"Yeah," said one of the others. "Good one."

"Good one," echoed Atticus. "Well, I don't know about you guys, this is all very amusing and all that, but I could do with another drink." He waved his glass, which was still very much half-full.

"I don't think you're hearing me," said Ray Winstone, coming even closer. "He's not hearing me, is he lads?"

"Oh I am," Atticus assured him. "Loud and clear. Very...." his voice tailed off.

Just as he was absolutely sure he was about to be on the wrong end of a huge and well-aimed punch, he heard the door open behind him, followed by the most musical sound in all Christendom.

"Sweetie! What *are* you doing out here?"

The world turned on its head, and he found himself looking at Laura.

His first thought was that she looked even more like a goddess than she had at the Dorchester. She *was* a goddess. Her astonishing body was encased in a floor length turquoise satiny dress with a fishtail train, and no straps. He wondered if it was usual for a man to wonder how a dress was staying on, rather than simply hoping it would not. Her platinum hair was piled on top of her head with what looked like peacock feathers entwined in it, and she had enormous blue gemstones suspended from her ears.

"Thanks boys," she said, waving an elegant hand in the direction of the heavies, "I think we can handle things here." The three seemed to melt away, heading for the small back staircase, and sinking out of sight.

"Christ, what are you drinking?" she said to Atticus, grabbing his glass and taking a generous slurp."

"Actually, that's not too bad," she admitted after a moment. "But I think we can do better." And she led him by the hand back into the drawing room.

Whereas a moment ago, he had been looking at a wall of people's backs, now with Laura by his side, the bodies parted ahead of them, and gasps of curiosity and admiration could be heard in the air around him.

"Are you terribly bored?" Laura whispered in his ear, "These people are a bit - you know."

"I *don't* know actually," said Atticus, "I was wondering though... who *are* they?"

"Oh," said Laura, waving her beautiful hands airily, "they're just rich people. Lovely, lovely rich people. A bit serious though, don't you agree?"

And she laughed the laugh of Tinkerbell, risen from the dead, at the clap of a child's hands.

"More money than taste most of them of course," she added conspiratorially, "Not like you."

"Well I certainly don't have *this* kind of money," Atticus admitted, staring at a Rolex Oceanmaster bigger than a snooker ball, on a nearby wrist.

"And that, my lovely is because you..." Laura put her pretty face so close to Atticus's that he could see a light dusting of foundation on her cheek, "...are one of life's good guys."

"Of course it all went tits up in 07," said someone very loudly, "Fools lost millions. Hardly my fault I said, greed will have its day!" There was a huge guffaw of laughter.

"And besides," said an altogether different voice, in a whisper which was at least as audible as the bellowing, "I had already told him, if you get picked up, I don't know you, I was never here."

One of the men turned round and looked directly at Atticus. He frowned, as if trying to work something out, and then turned back, put a hand on his companion's shoulder, and said something under his breath before they both moved carefully away.

I'm just being paranoid, Atticus decided. He was still shaking slightly after he had accidentally shared a precious moment with gangland's answer to the Three Degrees by the back stairs. What *was* in that tarpaulin?

"How have you been? Since our lovely lunchette?" Laura was asking. Somehow two more generous drinks had appeared.

"Oh, Good. Good," Atticus said, " I spoke to my sister actually. She remembers you of course."

"Does she sweetie? Does she? How cool!"

38

"You might have been in her year. She's older than I am of course."

The slightest hint of a frown crossed Laura's lovely face.

"Oh well, I probably wouldn't then. What was her name again?"

"Hilly," said Atticus helpfully.

"Of course. Fab girl! Loved her to bits at school. Wasn't she the head girl? I was so jealous of her! We all were you know."

Hilly, once almost thrown out of the school for organising a pyjama-clad demonstration against the exclusion of women from the Garrick Club, had certainly never been head girl.

"Absolutely," he said, forgiving Laura instantly as her long eyelashes almost blew him over.

"Now, come with me," Laura said, placing her arm on his sleeve. He could almost feel its heat wrapping him up like a duvet, "I want you to meet some *people*."

There followed a series of handshakes, as people reluctantly tore themselves away from staring at Laura to look briefly at Atticus before returning their eyes to her.

"This is Tommy. He's in Shipping."

"These reprobates, are Phil and Donny. They're Italian, so don't believe a word they say!"

"This is Stan. His real name's unpronounceable. *Russian.*" She whispered the last word into Atticus's ear.

"This is Christos. He's in oil. Christos, you must do something for Atticus, He's frightfully clever."

Atticus noticed she didn't introduce him to any of the women, although there were plenty of them.

"Do you know any of the women?" he asked, after yet another group had been completely ignored as Laura waved them aside to reach another target

"Heavens no Darling," she said, "They're just guests. If you see what I mean. For the *evening.* Better dressed than we are," she added, with a slight note of frustration. "Onward!" She steered him out of the room altogether and down the main staircase. The nude statue regarded Atticus coolly as if daring him to place his hand on her again.

"Now." Laura said, as they stood on the lower landing. "A little reward for all that politeness I think." And she kissed him. Totally, properly, completely, and for really quite a long time. It would have been ungentlemanly not to respond with enthusiasm.

As she drew back, he saw that she was frowning. He panicked.

"Sorry," he said.

"Don't be," said Laura in a strange voice. "You know, you're really rather good at that."

A door opened across the landing and a harassed looking man came out, backwards. He almost stumbled into Atticus, before turning and scurrying away.

"Oh dear," said Laura. "It looks as though Boran's being a bit of a brute today!" Taking Atticus's hand she pulled him gently but firmly through the open door and shut it behind them.

"Laura," said a velvety voice from deep inside the room, "How lovely you look."

"Babe," purred Laura.

Atticus looked round. He could hear the voice, he could feel that there was someone else in the room with them, but he couldn't actually see anything except thick brocade furnishings. Miles and miles of gold piping and cord, swags, tails, overstuffed cushions and brass lanterns made what must have been quite a big room feel a bit like being in a four poster bed. But not as intimate.

A faint smell of cigar smoke rose around them. Atticus struggled not to cough, fearing he would sound like a kid having his first cigarette behind a bike shed. He looked at Laura who seemed to be wrapping herself in the strands of smoke as if it were wool.

"And this," said the invisible man, "Is the man you told me about?"

"This is Atticus," she said, "I'm so glad you two lovely guys could meet! Boran, this is Atticus, Atticus, this is Boran!"

"Hi," said Atticus into the darkness.

"These *bloody* parties, Laura, you know I hate them," said the voice, unexpectedly, "Why the hell you keep bringing all these terrible people together I can't think. Don't you hate this sort of thing Atlas?"

"Er, well, Atticus actually. Although it doesn't matter of course...er..it was kind of Laura to ask me... I..er, to be honest I haven't really been to... I mean.." mumbled Atticus, his voice fading away.

"Of course you do," said the voice. "You haven't even got a drink. Laura? Get us both a bloody drink will you? A proper drink, not that terrible stuff you're serving out there."

Laura moved across the room to a cabinet where there was a large collection of decanters, and poured generous measures of something into two huge glasses. She handed one to Atticus and he almost dropped it, so heavy was the weight of the crystal. He put his nose to the glass and came close to passing out with the fumes. He wasn't used to whisky at all, and this was a whole lot more powerful than a snifter of Johnnie Walker at the end of a bad party.

"Better," said the voice, and Atticus assumed the mysterious Boran had received his drink as well.

"Now why don't you both sit down, and you can tell me all about yourself."

Laura beckoned to Atticus, and they moved closer to the source of the voice. As the smoke cleared, he saw a large Middle-Eastern-looking man with very thick dark hair and a 1970's moustache, not unlike the one he had seen on the way in to the party, sitting in a massive velvet-upholstered armchair. He was wearing what looked like a dressing gown, made in a striped, shiny material. The cigar smouldered in a glass ashtray beside him.

"Well, this is....well....." said Atticus.

"We were at school together!" said Laura. "As I told you babe, Atticus is *very* clever. I met him again recently. Quite by chance really, we sort of bumped into each other. Didn't we Atticus?"

There was a pause. Being phoned quite out of the blue and invited to go to one of the smartest restaurants in London for lunch, by a woman you hadn't seen for twenty years was hardly 'by chance' On the other hand it seemed rude to contradict her.

"Well yes..." he said eventually.

"Laura, you are ridiculous sometimes. You have never bumped into anyone in your whole life. That's one of the reasons why I admire you. Nothing ever happens to you by chance."

Immediately a tide of conflicting thoughts swept through Atticus's head. He *admired* her? Was he her boyfriend? Did Boran think that he, Atticus, was a rival? Was there going to be some kind of showdown?

Perhaps he was her brother. But then again, not with that hair, that moustache. Laura was as pale as a ghost, Boran looked like Omar Sharif.

"Well, sort of by chance," Laura was saying. "I've known Atticus for ever. I thought you should meet him."

Why? thought Atticus? Were they worried about being short of wedding guests?

"He got in alright then," said Boran.

Laura laughed. "Of course," she said. "I *told* you."

Told him what? thought Atticus. He wasn't sure he relished having obviously been the subject of some advance conversation. He feared his reputation may have gone instead of him.

"Excellent," said Boran.

Atticus was completely lost. What the hell were they talking about?

"It's been good to meet you," said Boran.

Atticus realised he was being dismissed. He got up, still clutching the whisky.

"Well..yes.. thanks.. It's been...."

"Look after her," said Boran.

Did Boran think *he* was *Laura's* boyfriend? Could you become someone's boyfriend by default?

"Of course," Atticus said politely.

"See you soon," said Boran, who had disappeared again behind another cloud of blue smoke.

"Bye Babes," said Laura, who clearly wasn't coming out with Atticus.

He left the room and finding himself back on the landing, grabbed an ornate pineapple-carved banister rail to steady himself on the way up again.

"You might want to go easy on the Sazerac," said one of a group of several men standing by the door to the room where the party was still clearly in full swing. "If you're not used to it." And they laughed.

To spite them Atticus stood up to his full height of five foot nine, and threw the remainder of his drink down his throat. Shaking his head, in an attempt to stifle the peal of bells which accompanied the alcohol hitting his bloodstream, he nodded to the men, and strode confidently towards the door, missing it by a good foot and hitting his head on the frame.

Ignoring their laughter, he tried again, and made it into the room.

Chapter Four

"Atticus? Can I ask you something?"

"Sure.....what?"

"Do you know anyone, whose name begins with a letter before H? Like someone called Anthony? Or Bella? Charles? Fenella?"

"Um............"

"Because the thing is, much as I adore you, I'm a bit fed up with being woken up at two thirty in the morning, after, let me see, forty five minutes sleep, because my name is the first one on your speed dial list."

"Yup. Right. Fair enough."

"I mean, you must know some other people you could talk to when you're drunk?"

"Yeah. Right. Yeah. Loads. Loads of them. You're right. I'll call them. One of them. Someone else. You're *so* right. Thanks."

"Goodnight little brother."

"Yeah. Absolutely."

Chapter Five

"Atticus?"

"Yeah.Hi!.....It's me!"

"Atticus."

"Yeah. The thing is........."

".............."

"Well, Sorry. "

".............."

"It's just that I was thinking...I mean, now that I'm a grown adult, I'm not really your *little* brother am I?"

"That depends how you look at it. Right now I'm looking at it from the point of view of a woman who has been phoned several times in succession in the middle of the night because her brother still doesn't know what to do with his life."

"Good point. OK. Night then!"

"Goodnight Atticus."

Chapter Six

"The way I see it old man, you can't go wrong. You're single, you're young. *Ish*. You're free." Hal said the following Sunday, as the two men set about producing the lunch.

Atticus's brother-in-law spoke with something approaching regret, as he hoisted a very competent-looking roast leg of lamb out of the oven, basted it, and replaced it, somehow managing to top up Atticus's glass and his own with a generous quantity of Merlot as he did so.

"But you've got to agree, it does sound a bit odd," Atticus said, "I mean, she's an angel. And I'm an out of work, ex-something or other, with a bit of inherited cash I did nothing to earn, and no prospects at all."

"Agreed," said Hal, "Yup, you're right. Hopeless."

"She knows all these fabulously rich people, who stand about in corners and whisper about Russia and Billion-dollar brokerage, and private jets."

"You can talk the talk," said Hal, "You read history at Cambridge. You're as clever as the next man in any room I've ever been in. You shouldn't let a load of bollocks-speak get to you."

"The problem is, I get the impression that it isn't bollocks," said Atticus. "When they speak it. I think might just be real."

"Who'd know the difference?" said Hal, chopping handfuls of fresh mint, "A real yacht is the same as a made-up yacht when you're standing in the checkout queue in Tesco."

"So you think I should go on with it then?" Atticus asked.

"Let me get this straight," said Hal, "You want me to tell you whether you should continue to date an insanely fit bird, who hangs out with billionaires, and is really into you. You're asking me, a forty-five year old fat bloke, the father of satanic twins, with a regularly overheating wife, sorry Hils but there it is...," Hal raised his eyes in silent nod to his wife who was at that very moment negotiating a truce between warring factions in the Gaza Strip that was the nursery, "You're asking *me*. Right?"

"Oh I don't know," said Atticus, "You're right. I'm worrying about nothing."

"Wrong," said Hal, "You're worrying about something. Something that most blokes would mortgage their souls for. Pass me that balsamic would you?"

Hilly came into the kitchen bearing one of the twins, who regarded her uncle with a tear-stained face, weighing up whether he was worth a punt for a handful of chocolate buttons.

"Hi Hun," said Hal happily, kissing his wife, "I've done the meat and the sauce, want me to knock up a pud? How about my patented toffee and banana brulee?"

"You guys," said Atticus sadly, suddenly unable to bear the chaotic,   slightly sticky and blissful harmony a moment longer and leaving the room.

"He's wondering if he should pursue the Lovely Laura," Hal said to Hilly quietly.

"Oh God. What did you say?"

"I said why not? Anyway from what I hear, she's the one dong the pursuing."

"Hal! Do you think it's wise?"

"Look the poor bugger hasn't been out with a girl since, well you know, since what happened with Flora happened. This could be just the thing to get him back on the horse, so to speak. Anyway, by the sounds of her, she won't be around for long."

"I should hope not. I certainly wouldn't want Laura Hutchinson to be my sister-in-law."

A few hours later, the remnants of the excellent lamb and the last of the toffee and banana pudding safely stowed away, and the twins briefly asleep in beanbags in a corner of the kitchen, Hal, Atticus and Hilly sat peacefully in the drawing room with the papers, murmuring companionably from time to time, or reading small snippets of news to one another.

"Where's the Society Gossip page of this?" said Hal suddenly, waving the *Sunday Times*.

Hilly frowned at him meaningfully.

"I think it must have dropped out. At the newsagent," she said.

Chapter Seven

Mondays were still the worst. Working Mondays had been hard enough, the blissful freedom of a lovely weekend spent doing nothing but reading and thinking, brought to an abrupt end by another dark and early start, the increasing pressure of work, the knowledge of a long week ahead.

But unemployed Mondays were worse. Knowing that everyone else was going somewhere, with something to do, that the world was continuing to turn while he was standing still, on the outside, useless, contributing nothing. And still the long week loomed ahead.

"Lucky you," they all said, "All that time to do all the things you've always wanted to do."

The trouble was, that now Atticus had the time, he couldn't think of a single thing he wanted to do.

Things happened without him. They happened near him, round him, occasionally *on* him, but almost always, without him having anything to do with it.

He was an empty shell, a space where people decided to put things, feelings, ideas, deciding for themselves who he was and what he wanted. It was a kind of invisible.

Perhaps that was why Laura had been such a surprise. Men like him didn't get girls like Laura Hutchinson.

Anyway, it was academic now. She wouldn't call him again, not after the whole mumbling, shuffling, backing-in-and-out-of-rooms thing. It had been almost a week since the party, and he had almost begun to wonder if it had ever happened at all. He suspected that if he went back over to Mayfair, found the same street, and walked up and down, he would find all the houses were just houses, none of them hiding a secret inner world, full of secrets and whispering people and strange imported booze.

He wondered whether it was too early to go out for lunch. Perhaps he would see someone he knew, or make a new acquaintance browsing in a bookshop. Maybe an idea for a novel would come to him while he walked by the river, or maybe he would be run over by a coach load of American tourists and all the decisions would be made for him.

He put his coat on. Anything was better than staring at the walls counting the minutes until he could decently pour himself a glass of something nice and watch *Bargain Hunt*.

The buzzer by the front door went, making him jump. It was a rare sound, and Atticus had to concentrate for a minute to remember how to respond to it. The pale sweaty face of the doorman loomed into view on the little screen, over-exposed by the fluorescent bulb above his head, giving him a ghostly look.

"There is a delivery," Andrzej said in his thick Polish voice. "You'll 'ave to come down."

A moment later, as the lift doors opened into the foyer, Atticus got the impression of a heavy man in motorbike leathers leaving the building. Andrjez handed him a large heavy white envelope, with his name written on it in large and impressive handwriting.

Impulsively Atticus lifted it to his nose, and breathed in. It was an entirely new scent, and yet joyfully familiar.

"Marc Jacobs," said Andrjez without looking up again. "Letter. He smell of Marc Jacobs. Very expensive."

"Laura," Atticus wanted to say in return. "It smells of Laura."

A letter such as this deserved a scenic backdrop he thought, as he ran up the stairs, unable to bear the wait for the lift. If he had a great brandy, or champagne, he might just have poured it first, but he didn't have either. Instead he went over to the window with the precious letter, not stopping to take off his jacket or close the front door behind him.

The envelope was sharp and stiff, as the flap released its grip it could have cut a suicidal man's wrists. A heavy piece of card came quietly out, accompanied by a thinner, coloured folder with a British Airways logo on it.

The folder held an open-ended, first class return ticket, in his name. The card appeared to be the confirmation of a hotel reservation, although it was written in Italian, embossed in gold.

The Campanile Grande, Calle Tiepolo 1364, Venice, Italy and a date and time. Atticus looked at his watch, realising it was just three days away.

He turned it over. On the back, in her extraordinary handwriting, Laura had written:

There's a Party! There are people I'd like you to meet. I'll tell you where to go when you get here. Please come. We could have so much fun Darling. Laura. xxxxx

The 'L' was interspersed with swirls of the pen, and small intricate hearts and flowers.

"Hopelessly affected," he could hear Hilly saying in his head.

He was hopelessly excited.

"What are people wearing in Venice in the Spring?"

"Atticus?" Hilly's voice, thick with sleep, sounded strange as she retrieved her phone from underneath Postman Pat, deep in the heart of the house.

"Oh God Hilly - *Sorry!*" said Atticus. "I waited as long as I could. I thought this might be a good time to call. You know, after lunch, before baths?"

"Oh yes it's probably fine," said Hilly, "I'm not actually sure what time it is."

"It's four. Ish"

"Oh hell is it? It was half past three last time I looked. That means I've lost half an hour. Hell knows what the twins will have done in their bedroom."

"Do you have to go and see?"

"No," said Hilly with a sigh, "I can hear them singing, so they aren't dead, and I can't face any more detail right now. Go ahead."

"What are they singing?" asked Atticus.

There was a silence, and he could hear a sort of warbling in the distance. He smiled at the thought of his nieces, singing in their beds.

"I think it's *Nessun Dorma* from *Turandot*" said Hilly drily.

"Of course it is," said Atticus. "I recognised it instantly. None Shall Sleep. Most appropriate. Look - about Venice."

"*Venice*? What about it?"

"I'm going to it. Tomorrow. What shall I wear?"

"Atticus, I've no idea. My sartorial decision-making is restricted to whether I can get away with something for a third time without washing it, and whether it will do up across my massively overflowing tummy and my disastrously droopy tits. I daresay if you put your mind to it, you'll have the right thing. It's warmer there than here I think. But not hot. Ask Ma, she always knows about weather."

"I haven't got that long," said Atticus, "And I only want to know about Venice, not climate change in Costa Rica or melting icecaps in the Antarctic. You know what she's like. Anyway she's *painting*."

"Good point. I'd forgotten she was back at work again. You're right, you can't possibly disturb the muse."

Hilly, suddenly woke up properly. "Anyway, what do mean you're going to Venice?"

"Laura asked me," said Atticus. "There's a party apparently."

"In *Venice*?" Hilly was incredulous, "That girl certainly gets about. I haven't been to a party since New Year's Eve and that was the people next door, whose idea of Hogmanay is sherry, and a full-length screening of the footage they took on their holiday to Croatia. I don't mean to rain on your parade kiddo, but is it *wise*?"

"You're right of course," said Atticus, "But Laura's sent me a ticket, and a hotel reservation at the Campanile Grande, and it seems like a lot of trouble to go to if you're not serious about someone?"

"The *Campanile Grande*? Look Atticus, the thing is...." said Hilly.

"What?"

There was a silence.

"Nothing," said Hilly. "Go for a light jacket and trouser thing, a second jacket, a couple of white shirts, a sweater, probably your DJ and a pair of respectable swimming shorts. That should cover it. Oh, and loafers. They all wear loafers in Italy."

"Thanks Hills," said Atticus, "Look are you OK? You sound strange."

"I *am* strange," said Hilly, "I've been taken over by aliens. They've drained me of all my blood, and replaced it with Ribena. Then they spat shepherds' pie all over me so I can't ever go out, and now they shout at me for twenty three hours a day. I tell you, the CIA should consider twin torture as an alternative to waterboarding."

"Can I do anything to help?"

"Of course not. Go to Venice dear one, play in gondolas on the Grand Canal and kiss masked beauties in doorways, and drink Bellinis at Harry's Bar. Oh, and swing by the Lido on the vaporetto and tell Bill Nighy I love him."

"Bill Nighy? What makes you think he'll be in Venice?"

"Whenever I dream of Bill Nighy," Hilly said firmly, "Which is *often*, he is in Venice. And whenever I dream of Venice, which I do almost as often, Bill Nighy is definitely there."

"I'll tell him," said Atticus. "You know he's not good enough for you, don't you?"

"Bye, Bill Nighy," said Hilly as sleep threatened to overtake her again.

Atticus spent a pleasurable evening packing his clothes into the previously unused holdall which Hilly had given him for his birthday a couple of years ago.

"For your honeymoon," she had said. But that had been so long ago. The bag had never left his apartment.

He ran his hands over its pleasingly distressed leather, and was thankful for his sister's impeccable taste if not for the sentiment which had seemed so thoughtful at the time and now seemed like a reproach.

He packed according to Hilly's list, apart from the loafers because he wasn't entirely sure what constituted a loafer and whatever it was, he was pretty sure he didn't have any. If everyone really was wearing them in Venice, he told himself, he could probably find somewhere to buy them.

The bag, even when he had packed everything he could find that was respectable enough, still looked a bit meagre. He rummaged in one of the dozen or so boxes of books he had stowed in the apartment's completely unused second bedroom and found his copy of Hemingway's *Across the River and Into the Trees,* tucking it into the holdall's inside pocket next to his washbag. He had always found a book most useful for disguising the fact that you have no idea where you are or what you should do.

Chapter Eight

Hilly pulled her coat round her, and twisted this way and that in front of the long mirror in the hall. She frowned at her reflection, and then again at the reflection of the minefield behind her. The twins had been playing safari parks, and the stairs were littered with soft toys, primary coloured plastic buckets, sticks and for some reason, courgettes.

Upstairs Hal was explaining in words of one syllable the necessary crowd control techniques to next door's teenage daughter who had kindly offered to look after the twins while Hilly went out.

It all felt very odd, and she hadn't left the house yet. The fact that it was a last-minute decision didn't help. Since having the twins everything had to be planned well in advance, due to the sheer number of things which had to be thought about, risk-assessed, mopped up, wiped down, and put into bags before opening the front door.

Just having real shoes on was a novelty. Her feet had become so used to being thrust into worn-out deck shoes that they were already protesting against being squeezed into a medium heel. She was wearing a skirt too, with a once-pale-pink shirt and a once-decent jacket. All things which had become impossible to put on with a small child hanging on to each arm. She had taken the opportunity to throw her usual sweatshirt and stretch jeans into the washing machine and now she felt rather as she imagined the twins did when Sheepish the Sheep or Churchill the duck absolutely had to be wrestled from their owners and shown the Persil.

"Wow," said Hal, coming down the stairs with a basket, collecting the safari park residents as he did so, "You look fabulous."

"Don't be daft. I look like a fat old person trying to get into clothes she wore when she was young and thin," said Hilly gloomily. "I've had this skirt for ten years."

"Well I've always liked it," said Hal loyally. "I tell you what, why don't you treat yourself while you're in town? I reckon we could run to a bit of a spree. As long as you steer clear of Joseph and Prada."

Hilly looked at her husband. He was such a good man, she thought. None of her friends' husbands would be anything like as long-suffering. When they'd found out that their much longed-for first baby was going to be twins, he'd even altered his practice so he could do all his casework at home, just going to the office for the face-to-face consultations with the children he counselled. And she wouldn't mind betting that the majority of his clients weren't anything like as demanding as the twins.

Now he spent all day talking troubled and sad youngsters out of bad or self-harming behaviour and he had to come home to a wife who hadn't brushed her hair in a fortnight and two mercurial children whose idea of a welcome home was to climb up the curtains and insist they were chimpanzees, refusing to respond to anything other than monkey noises.

He was far more patient than she was, too, and over the five years they had been married had developed an almost sixth sense about when she was just about coping and when she had just had enough.

All of which made it much harder to deceive him.

"I'm not sure I'll have time for shopping," she said, "I"m meeting Maggie in Knightsbridge at 12.30 and I haven't seen her for ages so she's sure to have plenty to talk about. Which is good, because I'll probably fall asleep in my spaghetti, without two screaming baked-bean-throwing children to keep me awake."

Hal laughed. "Perhaps you should ask the management to sit you next to the most troublesome family they can find," he said. "Just so you don't feel homesick. Well look, if Maggie does want to hit the shops, don't feel you have to get straight back. I can manage, I only have to be out for a couple of hours and Janice is here."

As he said the words there was a loud animal wail from upstairs. Hal and Hilly looked at each other, waiting to see what happened next.

"Sorry!" shouted Childminder Janice from upstairs, "That was me! I stubbed my toe on the sodding pirate ship."

"Quick," said Hal, opening the front door and ushering his wife out. "Off you go while there's still time. Let me know when you make it over the border, and whatever you do, keep on running."

Hilly felt even worse.

As she walked the half mile to the station, she wondered why she hadn't just come out and told Hal what she was doing. After all, he hadn't exactly said she shouldn't. But she knew that he thought she was just stirring up trouble. "Atticus has to make his own mistakes," Hal had said.

"I just feel responsible," Hilly had said, "I know it's stupid, and he's old enough, if not wise enough, to sort out his own life. It's just that he's had such a rough time recently, and I'd hate him to be disappointed again."

"You've aways looked out for him Hils," Hal had said, "and he knows you're there for him. You don't have to keep proving it. And it's not as if you haven't got enough to do."

As if to prove a point one of the twins had started to splutter and the red wax crayon couldn't be found and various versions of the Heimlich manoeuvre had to be performed before the crayon was found in a plant pot and the cough had been proven to be the result of too much juice going down the wrong way, and by the time it had all been sorted out, largely by most of the juice returning at speed, Hilly somehow hadn't explained her plan. Now it was time to go, and she'd just said the first thing which came into her head.

Which was that she fancied a lunch in Harvey Nichols with a girlfriend, and not that in fact, she would be nowhere near Knightsbridge but was heading instead into the City to a dingy wine bar round the corner from her old Chambers.

She texted Maggie while standing on the platform, to fill her in, in case Hal rang. Anything could happen with the twins, and she had to be sure Maggie would cover for her.

Hilly's phone beeped as she put it back in her pocket.

At airport. Can't believe it's 4 real. Maybe my life is picking up! Ax

Hilly texted back.

Am Green with Envy. May be pureed peas. Go Bro! Hils x

Chapter Nine

Atticus queued for about half an hour behind slightly overexcited teenagers, honeymoon couples, and a woman who refused to be separated from her hairdryer, before getting to the check-in desk.

Putting his holdall on the weighing belt, the check-in operator, whose name badge declared her name to be Priya, looked several times at his ticket and then back at him, which made him a little nervous.

"You know you shouldn't really be here," she said cheerfully.

That was it. He knew it. It had all been some kind of mistake. Typical. Why should anyone as beautiful as Laura want to have anything to do with him. Why would *anyone* ever buy him an air ticket to Venice?

"Oh Right. Sorry," he said, reaching for the holdall. It had all been a cruel joke. Or a stupid misunderstanding. He would just have to go home, draw the blinds, and lie low for a week. Nobody would know. He could probably get a guidebook somewhere, read up about Venice, so he could talk about all the things he didn't do as if he had really done them.

The holdall moved along the belt away from him, and Priya tied a 'Priority Baggage' label on it before sending it with what looked like a loving little pat, on its way.

"There's a fast track queue for First Class passengers," she said to Atticus, "*You* don't have to wait."

She pointed across the concourse to a roped-off desk on an incongruous bit of carpet, where a tiny woman with massive amount of bouncy hair, wearing dark glasses and an extremely short skirt was being assisted with her diamante clutch bag by two airline staff, while the two heavy-set men who appeared to be accompanying her, loaded five or six trunks onto a trolley.

"She's a Sugababe," said Priya conspiratorially. "Or is she a Saturday? One or the other. Or a Pussycat Doll. Anyway, you're in good company."

She stamped Atticus's ticket, and handed it back to him with an even wider smile. "The First Class passenger lounge is through the double doors on the right, between Hermes and the Harrods outlet," she said, "Although I suppose you'll be shopping for the woman in your life when you get to Venice, won't you?"

Atticus looked at her but there seemed to be no trace of irony in her face.

"Have a good flight," she added.

There were two hours before the plane was due to leave. After the usual scuffles in the security queues, where he always worried that someone else would get through before him and accidentally put on his shoes, or his belt, he wandered about for a bit in Departures, looking in at the brightly lit interiors of the shops, and wondering who would pay £1000 for an executive briefcase.

It was as he was gazing at an impressive display of designer fragrances and wondering if he really should think about buying a present for Laura, that he thought he saw a familiar face, inside the shop.

Well not exactly a familiar face, in that it was not somebody he actually knew, but a man he had seen somewhere before. About six two, with broad shoulders and dirty yellow curling hair. He just couldn't quite put his finger on where. A co-incidence.

At the same time, a child riding on a wheelie suitcase cannoned into Atticus's legs, and when he stood up again, the man had gone, which was odd, because he hadn't noticed anyone coming out.

He went into the shop, and was immediately enveloped in a cloud of assorted high-end smells. He looked round, and realised he was the only customer in the place.

"Now Sir, What can I show you?" said a smooth voice, "Are you looking for something in particular?"

"That man," Atticus said, "The man who was in here a minute ago?"

"No," said the voice, "I think you must be mistaken, we've had a very slow morning actually, haven't we Quentin?"

"We have indeed Michael," said a second man, in a similar but slightly higher voice. "We haven't seen a customer for at least an hour. I was beginning to wonder if they'd evacuated the airport again!"

Both men laughed gaily, congratulating themselves on the joke.

"Now then, let's get to business, mustn't keep our customer waiting must we? Are you shopping for yourself, or for someone else? I *love* that jacket by the way, is it Paul Smith?"

"Well, I...er.. well maybe a present?"

"A gift? Of course. Now what do we know about the recipient?

Atticus pictured Laura, and was momentarily breathless, as he imagined her, this time, on a Venetian gondola, lying back on silk cushions, patting the seat next to her invitingly, while a gondolier in a striped shirt waited to propel them both down the Grand Canal. In this vision, Laura was wearing white, her long brown legs barely concealed by the layers of floating fabric, her hair ruffled by the breeze.

"She's lovely," he said without realising he had spoken.

"*She.*" Quentin said, apparently fighting some inner disappointment, "Of course. Now do we know what fragrance she wears? Have we got that far in our relationship?"

"Mmmm *so* important," said Michael, "So many people make the mistake of thinking they'll just be able to guess. *Dreadful* if you get it wrong."

"Oh yes, dreadful." agreed Quentin, "Can *ruin* a relationship from the start."

There was a slightly awkward silence. "It wasn't my fault," said Michael his face clouding, "I misheard you."

Atticus looked round the shop hoping for clues. Then suddenly, he had a brainwave. "Andrjez!" he said aloud.

Both men perked up. Atticus saw their renewed enthusiasm and felt he needed to act quickly. "Andrjez," he said again, "He's er..a friend. He knows my, well, my, other ...friend. I mean he doesn't actually know her, but he suggested, well anyway he seemed to think *Marc Jacobs?* Does that make sense?"

Quentin skipped towards a glass cabinet and began taking an assortment of coloured bottles out, placing them lovingly on the counter.

"Now," he said, "Would we be talking *Honey, Daisy Hot Pink, Dot*, or perhaps *Oh Lola?*"

"I love, love, love, *Oh Lola!*" said Michael.

Atticus looked confused. "I'm afraid I don't know," he confessed. "I'm a bit of a novice at all this. Are they ..." He searched for the right word, "... flavours?"

Both men laughed happily, in the face of an almost inevitable sale. "So *funny* sir! Fragrances, they're all signature fragrances by the great Monsieur Jacobs."

Quentin did little praising gestures with his eyes raised to heaven, while Michael started spraying testers onto little bits of card, and waving them under Atticus's nose.

"Now that's *Honey*," Quentin said, "*My* particular favourite. Lovely, I'm sure you'll agree, Pear, Mandarin, Peach Nectar, and just a hint of Vanilla."

Atticus breathed in deeply. The scent was pleasant, but sweet. It was a friendly scent, like a summer holiday, or a dessert, a mousse perhaps. Or a cake. But decidedly unfamiliar.

"No, that's not it I'm afraid," he said.

"Try this," said Quentin, advancing with a second strip of paper. "Now this, is *Daisy Hot Pink*. Strawberries, violet petals, gardenia, and a decent waft of birch and cedar wood."

Atticus sniffed the proffered tester strip, and shook his head. "Sorry," he said.

"Well then it's *my* turn," said Michael. He barely had to raise the paper in Atticus's direction, when he was immediately transported back to The Dorchester. He could see the curtains, the tablecloths, he could taste the souffle, and above all, he could *feel* Laura.

"Pear, Raspberry, peonies, Cyclamen, Sandalwood and.....Tonka bean!" announced both men in unison.

"That's it," said Atticus faintly, "Oh yes, that is definitely it."

"*Oh Lola* it is!" said Quentin, "Lucky, *lucky* girl! Now, shall I gift wrap it?"

Atticus was still struggling to concentrate. He walked to the door, hoping for some air to clear his head.

Which was when he saw the familiar man again. Or at least he thought he did. Tall, over six foot, with quite a lot of messy yellow hair, and an unhealthy pale complexion, wearing dark jeans and a black jacket, over a beige sweater and a blue shirt. Even Atticus knew that it wasn't a good combination. Apart from which he must be so hot.

Although, looking slightly more closely, Atticus decided the man might be Scandinavian. But that would make it even more unlikely that they had met before. The City wasn't without its share of European star players, but Atticus's crowd had been distinctly English middle-class types who had got lucky mainly because they couldn't think of anything else to do.

The yellow-haired man was standing by W H Smith, and appeared to be talking into his mobile phone. Where *had* he seen him before?

"Will that be all?" said Quentin, holding out a large and very beautiful parcel, wrapped in shiny foil with a huge silk bow.

"Oh, right. Yes of course." Atticus said, wondering how he was going to get the ostentatious package to Venice without crushing it or losing it.

"That's one hundred and thirty pounds," said Quentin.

"*How* much?" Atticus said in his head, "*How* much?" said an imagined Hilly, in his right ear, "*How* much?" said his mother in his left ear. He had to remind himself that Laura had paid for lunch at The Dorchester. And the party, And the air ticket. It was the least he could do. And his mother had always said one should never arrive anywhere without a present.

Seeing Atticus's raised eyebrows, Quentin added, "She will be *so* appreciative. Every woman loves to have her man buy her own, special fragrance!"

Atticus handed over his credit card.

"And where are we flying to this morning?" asked Michael, as Quentin managed the card machine.

"Venice," said Atticus, and watched as the two men exchanged glances over the till.

"If Sir is looking for a *loafer*" said Michael, looking down at Atticus's rather weatherbeaten brogues, "You might try Cassini, on the Rue D'Ivola"

Quentin slammed the till shut with rather more force than was necessary. "I am sure *Sir* knows how to find a good supplier of footwear," he said icily.

Michael escorted Atticus to the door of the shop. As he turned to go back inside, he leant towards Atticus's left ear.

"Ask for Jerome," he whispered.

By the time Atticus had got over to W H Smith, the yellow-haired man had gone, of course. He told himself he was imagining things, and bought a copy of *The Spectator*, the latest Donna Leon paperback and a large bar of his favourite brand of dark chocolate.

He sent another text to Hilly.

Wow. perfume's v £££ isn't it?

Hilly pinged back within a couple of minutes

Get on plane Keep out of shops. Unless shopping for beloved sister x

The flight was announced and Atticus made his way along miles of nylon carpet, through doorways, down stairs, along another corridor and into the boarding area. He handed over his ticket and his passport, and felt the familiar prickle of fear. Perhaps it was here they would discover he was a fraud, and throw him out.

The steward punched his boarding card and waved him through. "*You* can board when you're ready," he said, "You needn't wait to be called."

Two teenage boys behind him made 'oooo-er' noises.

Atticus sat down and opened *The Spectator*.

Chapter Ten

Barely still standing on a corner of Holborn and The Strand, The Cheese and Grain was as dingy as it had ever been. Somehow, the three years Hilly had been away had made it more romantic in her memory. She remembered dark corners, deep red leather seats, quaint victorian lamps and shiny ale pumps, but in reality it was just a sticky old pub which smelt, at this time of day, of loo cleaner and cheap furniture polish. There was a fruit machine in a corner and a greasy-haired teenager in a grimy sweatshirt was wiping things down with an equally grimy cloth.

As Hilly's eyes got accustomed to the gloom, she realised she wasn't alone in the pub. A very old man in a raincoat was perched rather incongruously on a bar stool at the far end of the bar, staring gloomily into a glass of what looked like whisky.

"Hello," she said, as it seemed rude not to.

"Pfffft..*Bugger,*" said the man into the drink.

Hilly stood at the bar for a while, but nobody came. Suddenly the man in the overcoat shouted.

"Will ye feckin' come on out here Mon! Woman'll be waitin' all *feckin'* day!"

A robust woman in a dressing gown appeared behind the bar.

"Oh," said Hilly, "Sorry to get you...er..up.... Look I'm early I know. I'm meeting someone at 12. Why don't I just take a seat and wait until you're ready to open? I'll be fine, Look...just.... Or I could wait outside?"

Hilly started to back out towards the door, before the overcoat man slammed the flat of his hand so hard on the bar his glass lifted off it.

"Fer feck's sake woman! D'ye want a drink or not!"

"Shutup Norman," said the woman in the dressing gown, mildly. Then she looked at Hilly. "I'm here now. What can I get you?"

Hilly had been going to ask for a glass of mineral water, but it seemed unlikely to be a popular choice at that point, so she ordered red wine instead. A glass the size of a vase appeared and the woman filled it from an unlabelled bottle.

"Great," said Hilly, "Thanks."

"Take the bottle," said the woman, leaving it on the bar before disappearing through a door at the back of the pub.

"D'ye want some help with that?" said Norman, indicating the bottle.

"Keep it," said Hilly hastily, as if it wasn't already too late.

The overcoat grabbed the bottle with one hand and drained the whisky from his glass with the other. Making a vague attempt at uniting the remaining wine with the now empty glass, he slid gracefully off the bar stool and seemed to be about to follow Hilly to her table.

Hilly's phone beeped and she pulled it out of her pocket grateful for the distraction. A picture of the twins wearing red plastic buckets on their heads like a pair of Tommy Coopers popped up on the screen, with a message from Hal.

Just Like that eh? have a good day. Love you H x

She laughed, and the overcoat continued towards her, sensing encouragement.

Fortunately at that point Graham arrived, bursting unceremoniously in and the overcoat, sensing the presence of authority, melted away.

"Bleedin' copper," she thought she heard him say under his breath. "They'll 'ave yer, soon as look at yer, so they will."

Graham looked suspiciously round. It was a pub he used regularly, but one could never be too sure who was listening in, and from time to time he had to relocate meetings, when some villain, or a member of the press, found out about it and moved in as well.

The coast seemed clear and he persuaded the landlady to relinquish the cigarette she was enjoying in the back yard to pull him a pint of beer.

"Now darling," he said, his familiar voice disappearing into the turned up collar of his overcoat, "What brings you all the way into grubby old Holborn after all this time?"

Hilly laughed. "You're so showbiz cop," she said. "I've missed you."

Chapter Eleven

The rest of the passengers were beginning to get edgy. Children were becoming fractious and running up and down trailing juice cups and blankets while anxious parents had already emptied their entire stock of amusing distractions onto the carpet, which was patterned with the airline logo. The repeated design was convenient for driving small trucks on, Atticus thought, admiring a veritable Grand Prix circuit being built by two small boys between the passport control desk and the water bottle dispenser.

He looked up to see a brown-haired man in rimless glasses looking rather intently at him.

Atticus nodded and the man looked away hastily, rummaging in a carrier bag for a pen and some scraps of paper on which he began scribbling, as if he had something terribly important to get down before it was too late.

There was something odd about him, Atticus thought, something which reminded him of....someone?

He told himself not to be ridiculous. He really was seeing ghosts now. First the man in the perfume shop and now this one. He tried to concentrate on the article he was trying to read but for some reason the words wouldn't make sense. He kept seeing faces swimming before him, men looking oddly at him, grinning, laughing, or just whispering to each other, but he couldn't quite place where he had seen them.

The departures board was still showing the flight as 'boarding' although it clearly wasn't. The plane was there, he could see it, right next to the window, its great fat nose almost touching the glass like a big dog trying to get into a room. The staff were busily shuffling bits of paper and picking up the intercom and putting it down again, arranging their evening's entertainment, and eyeing up the passengers.

He checked his phone but unusually, Hilly still hadn't responded to his last text, sent about fifteen minutes before. He had asked her if there was anything she would like as a gift from Venice, so it was even more odd that she hadn't replied. Perhaps she was out. She couldn't be out. She was *never* out.

He became aware of eyes on him again, and he looked up to see an airline steward approaching him.

"I wonder if you would come with me sir," the steward said in a low voice quite close to Atticus's ear. The eyes of the departure lounge upon him, he pulled together his shopping and his jacket and meekly followed, He just knew that they all thought he was responsible for the delay.

"My name is Ray-*mond,*" said the steward as they reached the desk, "I will be looking after you on the plane this afternoon. Please let me know if there's anything you need."

Raymond opened the door to the boarding tunnel just a faction and ushered Atticus through it, closing it behind them.

He sashayed the way down the tunnel and through the doors of the plane, where he turned left.

Atticus had never travelled First Class. He'd used business class before but only once or twice, and he had always been in the company of colleagues, so he had never really been able to enjoy it, having to pretend that he didn't notice or care either way, turning down the champagne and chocolate in favour of getting some sleep, because he was supposed to be so busy he needed to sleep whenever he wasn't actually in a meeting.

Raymond indicated an extremely comfortable looking seat, and drew a small curtain round it.

"May I hang up your jacket?" Raymond said, taking the rather creased linen from Atticus and putting it reverentially on a hanger. Then he picked up an intercom and spoke into it. "We're all clear here," he said, "Go ahead to board."

Then he turned back to Atticus "I hope you enjoy your flight," he said.

"Wait," Atticus said suddenly. Raymond stopped and turned back, raising an enquiring eyebrow.

"It's just, well, this special treatment... en said, "I'm not sure... I mean, I'm not sure you haven't got me mixed me up with someone else."

"Oh no sir," said Raymond with what might have been a laugh, but somehow wasn't, "We know exactly who you are. Glad to have you with us sir."

And he disappeared into a seething mass of hot, cross passengers heading towards him, greedy for their seats and for the adventure of flight.

A stewardess passed Atticus's seat and put a huge gin and tonic, complete with ice and lime on the table in front of him. He didn't remember ordering it, and the experience so unnerved him that he drank it.

After a while, he was joined in the First Class cabin by a honeymoon couple who were virtually undressed by the time they sat down, and clearly had eyes for nobody but each other, rummaging and stroking, and making alternate slurping and squeaking noises, while shedding confetti along with their clothes. He caught the eye of the bride, as she passed, a striking brunette with a lot of extremely good make-up and a diamond ring the size of a cup cake on her finger. Rather unnervingly, she winked at him.

Up ahead, the tiny pop star disappeared behind her curtain, and could just be seen through a gap, changing into a pair of silk pyjamas and a face mask. Water was brought, enormous shades found and put on, and she wrapped herself up in a huge cashmere blanket.

For a three hour flight? She must be exhausted Atticus thought. Not from the travelling, but from all the effort it clearly took to be *her*.

It was about then that he noticed the first man from the airport, the one with the yellow hair. He was carrying his jacket, but was still overdressed by several layers. He walked up the aisle towards Atticus's seat, and stopped.

Atticus looked up and smiled politely. "Good Afternoon," he said cheerily, hoping the man would remind him where they had met before."I see you're going to Venice too then?"

The man moved on, and took his seat a few rows ahead, without speaking or looking back.

As the plane taxied down the runway, Atticus wondered again why Hilly hadn't responded. He sat back and tried to feel excited about his trip. If anyone had asked him a week ago, whether he would be drinking extremely good gin in First Class on his way to a party in Venice with Laura Hutchinson, he would never have believed it. Maybe things really were beginning to look up. Maybe it finally was his turn.

Chapter Twelve

Graham finished his third pint and stood up. "I have to go," he said apologetically. "A case. You know how it is. I'm due in court this afternoon, and some hard-nosed posh bird in a wig will be giving me the third degree. *Sorry..*" he added, looking at Hilly. "Not you. You were different. I wish they were all like you."

"Soft, you mean," she said smiling.

"No, not that. You were good. Really good, It's just that we always knew where we were with you. Nowadays these young ones, they come straight out of law school, they know all the rules, all the cases, all the detail, but they don't know what real life is like. Out there at the sharp end. They can't see beyond the legal jargon and case files, to where the people are."

"I *think* there's a compliment in there somewhere," Hilly said. "So is there anything you can do?"

Graham patted the notebook he had put back in his pocket. "Leave it with me," he said, "I have to say, from what you've told me, I expect its all a storm in a teacup. He wouldn't be the first man to fall for someone out of his league. Perhaps he's just looking for a way back to reality, after all that sad business."

"That's just what Hal said," admitted Hilly. "But I'm not sure Atticus ever *did* reality. And I'm not sure *she* represents it either."

"But if you're worried enough to come to me, I'll do my bit," Graham said, "I'll ask around, see if anything comes up. If you're right to be suspicious, someone will know something. If there's nothing, well that's good news too."

"Unless it means I have to like her," said Hilly grimly.

"I don't suppose for one minute he would get really involved with someone you didn't like," said Graham "I wouldn't. You're the best judge of character I've ever met."

"You're forgetting Norbert Franklin," said Hilly.

"Ah yes," said Graham, "But then we were both wrong about him."

"Who would have thought that a mild-mannered ginger-bearded languages teacher would turn out to be the mastermind of a massive trafficking operation?"

"Who indeed?"

Graham held the door open and they both emerged into the afternoon, blinking, and slightly surprised that it was still daylight outside.

"You really have to go back to Cambridge this evening?" Graham asked, knowing the answer.

"You know I do," said Hilly. "The stickies will have eaten the childminder by now, and Hal will be exhausted."

"Shame," said Graham looking at Hilly. She had no idea how lovely she was, he thought. Not that she would look at a worn-out world-weary cop with a list of bad habits which included late night curry, too much cheap red wine and permanent insomnia. Not that she ever had. But that hadn't stopped him wondering if, one day, she might.

He kissed her on both cheeks, holding her for just a fraction longer than necessary.

"I'll let you know as soon as I hear anything," he said.

"Speak to *me* though," warned Hilly, "Not to Hal. He'd only worry."

Across the street, Moira Sanders who had once been on a fundraising committee for a children's hospice, of which Hilly had been the elected chairwoman, came out of the Pizza Express with a headhunter she had hoped would find her a top executive position to make her divorce less painful. The headhunter had not been encouraging, and Moira was not at that moment disposed to think well of anyone. She thought about waving to Hilly, but decided against it. She seemed rather busy, with that *man*.

Graham disappeared round the corner, taking the long route back to the police station, and Hilly decided to walk to the Tube.

Chapter Thirteen

The plane touched down gently. Marco Polo airport is on the Italian mainland, but as they had come into land there was so much water about Atticus wouldn't have been at all surprised to find that the runway itself was afloat. He was about to leap up and start the customary scramble to retrieve his jacket, but one look from Raymond who had miraculously appeared at his elbow was enough to keep him firmly in his seat.

Raymond then moved smoothly around the First Class cabin, unfolding things and reuniting passengers with their clothes, which in the case of the honeymoon couple took rather longer than anyone else.

"Your luggage will be taken directly to your water taxi," Raymond assured him quietly, "There will be no need to queue." He said the words with deep disgust, as though he was describing the process of dredging a swamp.

"Right," said Atticus, "Right, well thanks." Did one tip an airline steward? Who knew?

He waited until the babble of excited passengers died away behind him before getting up again. As he stood up, he saw the yellow-haired man with the black jacket do the same. Atticus hung about a bit, hoping to let the man pass but he seemed in no hurry to leave, instead clamping his phone to his ear. Atticus had the strange feeling that the man was merely pretending to take a call, the way you do when you spot someone in the street you don't want to see, or are too early for something and want to look as busy as the people who are always late and always telling you how they are so busy they are always late for everything, as if you couldn't possibly be busy enough if you were there on time.

Suddenly, two substantial men in black polo necked sweaters and heavy jackets thundered onto the plane and Atticus jumped backwards. One was taller than the other but each must have weighed more than fifteen stone and was built like a rugby prop forward. They wore sunglasses and carried walky-talky radios into which they were both growling. Atticus wondered if they were actually just speaking to each other.

He tried to fade into the background, which was awkward given the dimensions of the aeroplane cabin, and as they came towards him he could smell food, the combination of frying oil and sugar giving away a bad doughnut habit.

In another instant, the cabin was lit by a blaze of flashing light. At first he thought there had been an explosion, but then he realised he was still standing, and although the lights kept on flashing, they were coming from outside. He turned to look out of the window and saw about thirty or so paparazzi photographers standing on the tarmac right outside the door to the First Class cabin, all pushing and jostling one another and all with their huge cameras, and flashguns letting off a barrage of pops and flashes.

Almost blinded by the light, he looked back into the comparative gloom of the cabin and realised that the two heavies had thundered right past him, and were busy at the front. Then with a smoothness which belied their appearance, they swept the tiny pop princess, who was now wearing what looked like a taffeta evening gown, down the aisle between them, and out of the plane onto the steps.

"Cheyenne! Cheyenne!" He heard a massive roar from the pack of photographers, as the cameras went even more wild, and the tiny woman twirled round and round. Atticus remembered a music box of his sister's. When you opened the lid, a tiny little plastic woman in a ballet dress twirled just like that. Only the musical box woman was bigger of course.

"Wow," said Raymond, back at Atticus's shoulder. "Imagine being *really* famous."

Raymond spoke as though he would *really* like it.

"Imagine," said Atticus, without thinking. He couldn't think of anything he would like less.

"Anyway," said Raymond, seemingly launching himself out of the window of the castle of dreams he'd just built for himself and landing firmly on the earth, "Let's get you to your taxi."

He helped Atticus into the linen jacket which actually looked as though it had been pressed while it had been away, and tidied up his copy of the *Spectator*, handing it back neatly rolled up.

"Into battle," said Atticus, brandishing it as he stepped out onto the plane steps, ready to face the photographers.

The tarmac was deserted, and it was as if somebody had just wiped the sun off the surface of the sky. The air was thick and warm, and in the distance, he could see the last of the paparazzi cavalcade disappearing over the horizon, flickering and sparkling on its way.

He thought he felt someone behind him and turned suddenly, but there was nobody there. He made his way down the steps and heard the ground crew detach them from the body of the plane behind him, before they were towed away. Following a line on the tarmac ahead of him, he walked what seemed like a mile but was in fact less than a hundred yards to the terminal building. Boy, when the lights go out on celebrity you really notice the darkness, he thought. No wonder they all go to such lengths to keep the focus of attention on them.

The air was warm, and Atticus stood by the open door of the building for a little longer, taking in the joy of being in another city, another country. Beyond the airport lay adventure, and he hadn't had one of those for a long time.

He wasn't alone for long. As he went into the terminal, he saw crowds of arrivals, all jostling and pushing each other, restless after flights, anxious to get through the tricky bit of Customs, eager to be out and away in Venice - City of Dreams, la Serenissima. Fractious children whined, spoilt women tossed their hair about and rummaged in handbags for make-up to repair the damage done by cabin pressure, businessmen sighed and fired up their mobile phones.

From his vantage point he watched the baggage handlers shoving cases and boxes carelessly onto trailers, throwing the smaller items to each other with no thought to what might be inside them. Atticus had long since learnt it was better not to know some things, and what airport baggage handlers did with other people's belongings was clearly one of those things. He flinched, as a large box marked 'Fragile, this way up' landed heavily upside down on the tarmac.

Two large black limousines drew up beside a small private jet. Curious, he watched as a chauffeur in a braided hat got out, and opened the boot of one of the cars, before opening the rear passenger door. Then the chauffeur stood to attention by the car, as two other men came down the steps of the plane, followed by a third, in a fur coat and hat. Rather hot for fur, Atticus thought, wondering who he was, before he was escorted surprisingly forcefully by the two men, into the waiting car. A large amount of luggage was then loaded into the boot, and before Atticus could see anything else, both limos swept away.

Ahead of him the queue had begun to move and he edged forward, before a voice beside him said: "No no, I told you, you needn't wait! Your water taxi is ready for you sir! Your luggage is already aboard." Raymond, who looked rather affronted by Atticus's apparent reluctance to accept special treatment, took his arm and led him right past the remaining queue, much to the audible dissatisfaction of several fractious and impatient travellers.

Together they made it out into the late sun on the other side, and Atticus, who had rather hoped to arrive in Venice quietly, and thoughtfully, mindful of its centuries of history and its delicate elegance, found himself the focus of quite a lot of attention, not all of it positive.

Red-faced women shouted and pointed, there were shouts of 'who does he think he is?' and 'there is a queue you know' while a decidedly grubby child hit him on the knees with a plastic truck and shouted something which sounded suspiciously like "Naughty Bugger!" In the end Atticus was forced to be grateful for Raymond's help, as he was handed down into a water taxi, although it was only as its pilot pushed off from the dock that he realised he had ostensibly jumped another queue to get it. He looked back to see the child being lifted onto a vaporetto, together with assorted other travellers and their luggage.

Atticus noticed a cello sitting unattended on the quay, waiting its turn patiently, and wondered whose it was. Odd, not to have someone guarding it, even an ordinary cello was worth money.

But as the cello and the seething crowd receded into the distance, and the water taxi picked up speed, the pilot turned up the volume on the stereo and Atticus turned to look ahead at one of the loveliest sights he had ever seen.

Venice rose out of a light fog which was rising off the water, the strains of Bizet's *The Pearl Fishers*, one of Atticus's favourite pieces, filled the air

Laura should be here to see this, he thought, wondering where she was. She hadn't actually said she was going to meet him, but he was a little disappointed, if the truth be told. But then again, what could be more romantic than to meet later, in some pretty bar by a canal, two seasoned travellers, catching up with each other far from home. Or maybe she would be at the hotel, where they would be two nonchalant, wealthy tourists, promised the best the City could offer, ready to enjoy some elegant luxury together. Yes, that was it. She would be at the hotel.

The taxi chugged across the water and the City grew larger and more beautiful. Passing through the islands in the lagoon, Atticus tried to imagine what travellers from many centuries ago would have felt, on seeing the same sights. It was familiar in one way, the stuff of chocolate boxes, postcards, a thousand photographs, and yet in reality it was very, marvellously, different. Close up, Venice was a stranger, a ghostly figure in a faded dress, irresistible, beckoning like a siren. If she had been leading him to his death he would not have been able to do anything but follow, and as the little boat with its reassuringly polished teak decks got closer, and eventually turned into the Grand Canal, deep in the heart of the City, Atticus shivered, though he was not cold.

Venice was indescribably beautiful, but somehow, it was not entirely benign.

Chapter Fourteen

Narrowly avoiding bobbing gondolas, vaporetti full of tourists photographing the Rialto bridge, and the hosts of smaller and infinitely more prosaic boats which crossed again and again right in front of them, their captains seemingly oblivious to the ever-present danger of being T-boned by a waterbus, the taxi made its way up one canal and across another, the darkening streets on either side looking down at them, the water becoming blacker and blacker, until eventually it drew up at a small jetty marked by striped posts and flying ribbons. Atticus looked up at quite the most beautiful facade he had ever seen, a greying white wedding cake of a building with pillars and balconies galore. It was a palace.

A liveried doorman took a rope with one hand and held the other out to Atticus.

As his feet felt dry, if creaking, land, Atticus reached into his jacket pocket for his wallet to pay the taxi driver, but as he did so there was a roar, and the little boat sped away. The wash from his bow wave came up over Atticus's shoes, and the doorman tutted impatiently.

"Welcome to the Campanile Grande sir," he said, "I shall have your shoes looked after as soon as you get to your room of course." Under his breath, he uttered a stream of angry sounding Italian which Atticus was quite glad he didn't understand.

The inside of the hotel was as classically beautiful as the outside, but with a decidedly modern twist. Atticus felt sure he had stepped onto a film set. The foyer was busy with guests and staff mingling, luggage being whisked about and wildest dreams being met, yet the space was curiously silent, with no more than the gentle murmur of respect in the air.

If Hilly could see me now, thought Atticus, with a slight pang of homesickness. This was all very beautiful, but it was the sort of place where one could feel very alone. He wondered where Laura was and then caught sight of himself in one of a thousand mirrors and was glad she wasn't there to see what a crumpled mess he looked.

An elegant man in an impeccably cut grey suit and with the shiniest shoes Atticus had ever seen was walking towards him across the marbled floor. Atticus looked round but it seemed that he was the object of the man's attention. Surely this was the ambassador of something, or a member of the royal family here, he thought, but before he had time to step out of the way, the man held out a hand revealing just the right amount of perfect cuff and said, "Welcome Mr Drake, I am Anthony Antonioni. I am the hotel manager. We are delighted to have you with us here at the Campanile Grande, I hope you will let me know if there is anything, anything at all that you require while you are with us?"

He handed Atticus a large white leather wallet with the hotel's logo embossed in silver on the front.

"In here, you will find your room access code, and my personal mobile numbers, together with a number of suggestions which we hope you will find helpful while you are with us." he said.

With a very slight raise of a single eyebrow, Antonioni summoned an underling, who scuttled up to Atticus. "Marco will take you to your suite," he added, "If there's nothing else?"

Atticus took a deep breath. "Well," he said bravely. "I did wonder..."

Antonioni turned back, as if surprised that there could be a single thing he had not already thought of to make Atticus welcome.

"It's just..." Atticus said, in a voice which sounded decidedly squeaky in the vast space, "I was wondering, if someone had left... I mean, if there is any message, for me?"

Antonioni sighed, very gently. "If there is any message at any time," he said, "we will of course make you aware of it immediately. I shall check again for you, and Marco will come back to me in four minutes to establish whether or not any such message has been received."

"Thanks," said Atticus, feeling guilty for having offended the mighty Antonioni, and then cross with himself for being such a wimp. "I'm expecting news from Ms Hutchinson," he said firmly, "Ms Laura Hutchinson."

Was it his imagination, or did the slightest hint of an expression cross Antonioni's face? Something which looked a bit like, well, like *fear* to be honest.

"As I say Mr Drake," said Antonioni quietly, "I shall check immediately."

Marco started the journey across the massive pale floor towards the wide staircase, and Atticus, breathless from having the audacity to question

Antonioni, followed meekly, rather wishing he could disown the sadly single holdall Marcus was carrying in favour of a set of beautiful monogrammed cases, which seemed to be the right thing here. It was rather obvious he wasn't used this style of travel and also that he wouldn't be staying long.

"I may send for further luggage later," he said cheerfully to Marco, as they made their way along a corridor and then crammed themselves into a tiny, but bizarrely opulent lift. Marco, whose face was just inches from Atticus's chest nodded. "Si signore" he said, "non un altro violoncello spero."

"You speak English?" Atticus said hopefully.

"Si signore." said Marco.

"Only I thought you said something about a cello."

"Si signore, Violoncello. Is very heavy. Will not fit in lift."

"Right," said Atticus. "Well I can see that might be a problem. If I had one."

The lift doors opened and the two men stepped out into another corridor. Marco, fairly bounded along, as if he had been relieved of the weight of the nonexistent cello, only stopping when he reached the end.

"Your suite, Signore," he said. As he opened the door Atticus thought he heard another set of footsteps behind them, but when he turned there was nobody there. He shivered, though it was far from cold.

It was certainly the most beautiful hotel room he had ever been in. A huge white bed, layered with soft cotton, cashmere and satiny bedlinen, and piled high with grey and white striped silk cushions dominated one end of the room, and there was a wall of elegant wardrobes down one side, each one with a full length mirror set into its door, reflecting the view from the floor-to-ceiling windows opposite. And what a view it was. As Atticus stood looking out at the Grand Canal sweeping past just feet away, he was entranced by the bustling liquid thoroughfare which separated him from the beautiful buildings on the other side, where he imagined more beautiful people were standing at windows just like these, looking back at him.

Marco, having put the holdall squarely the middle of the floor looked hopeful for a while before realising Atticus had forgotten he was there and withdrew sulkily, leaving the door open. Atticus, startled by the noise of the boy's disgruntled tipless sniff, turned to see an altogether different man standing in the doorway.

That yellow hair, the puddingy complexion, the jacket-over-sweater combo, they were all becoming quite familiar by now. And yet there was something about the man's manner which was not altogether amicable.

"Hello again," said Atticus, "Can I help you?Are you looking for your room? Quite a coincidence, us both staying here isn't it?"

The man said nothing. Then he turned and left. Atticus, peering out into the corridor just a matter of seconds later, found the corridor empty, its miles of pale grey carpet untouched by ugly footprint. The man must be a faster mover than his size suggested.

Atticus locked the door of the room and decided to unpack to calm his nerves.

It didn't take long, the large Marc Jacobs present for Laura took up most of the room in the holdall, and it seemed the helpful Quentin and Michael in the airport shop at Heathrow had sprayed the packaging as they wrapped it, so now the whole of Atticus's limited venetian wardrobe smelt decidedly feminine. At least Laura would be able to find him if they lost each other in a dark street, he thought.

He found his phone and took a picture of the view from the window to send to Hilly, adding:

Wish you were here x

Was it wrong to wish your sister was with you in a wonderful extravagant romantic hotel? Odd perhaps. But she would love it. And he had to face facts, there wasn't anyone else. Not after Flora.

Except for Laura of course. And she was already here. At least he hoped she was. Probably already stretched out on a silk *chaise longue* in a room just like this, being served champagne in a tall crystal flute, with strains of Puccini playing in the background. He pictured her wearing a green silk dress, soft and flowing, just falling off one shoulder, and her hair piled up in a careless chignon, or whatever that bun thing was called. Marvellous. He should be there with her. But then, perhaps Laura wasn't alone? Perhaps Boran would be with her. He found that the very thought of them together hurt. Oh, the beginnings of love were so complicated. And it had been such a long time since he had been involved with love at all, never mind love so elaborate and confusing as this.

Having hung up his dinner suit and spare jacket, put his sweater, boxer shorts and socks all in separate drawers, and arranged his wash things around the enormous bathroom, he saw it was just past five. He had used up precisely fourteen minutes. He was just wondering what to do next when the internal phone rang.

"Signore Drake?" it was the voice of the manager, Antonioni. "I have the message you were asking about. It has *just* been received." Atticus thought he could hear the sound of an errant messenger being hit round the head for failing to deliver a message promptly. "You are requested to attend a reception at the Casa Miranda at six this evening. Your friend, Ms Hutchinson, she send special request that you be there. She says she will be waiting."

"Oh God, *Thank you!*" said Atticus with joy. "Oh that *is* good news. Marvellous." He was about to put the phone back in his pocket when he remembered he hadn't been given any directions. "Oh, could you just tell me, where *is...*" he said hastily, but Antonioni had rung off.

Atticus looked at his watch again. If he went straight out he would have time to wander a little before he found the Casa Miranda. He would enjoy the City for a while, and ask directions, maybe converse with locals get a real feel for the place.

Chapter Fifteen

He opened the wardrobe doors one by one, surveying the vast empty spaces until he found the one he'd hung his two jackets in. Then he took off the crumpled linen one he was wearing, and tried on both of the others. Neither looked remotely like it would be the right thing to wear in a cocktail bar in Venice. The invitation didn't warrant the dinner jacket, and the green tweed was frankly more Young Farmers than continental chic.

In the end he put the linen jacket on again, noticing that it still smelt slightly of aeroplane and hoping that it would be dark in the bar and nobody would notice the creases.

As he locked the door of the room carefully behind him, putting the heavy brass key in his inside pocket, he saw a beautifully dressed man with slicked back hair and a pale-blue cashmere pullover tied carelessly over the shoulders of a pink shirt walking along the corridor towards the lift. As the lift dropped smoothly to the foyer Atticus looked, as Englishmen in a lift usually do, first at the ceiling and then at the floor, avoiding eye contact with his elegant companion at all costs. Loafers. The man was wearing shiny tan slip-on shoes with tassells. Loafers.

There was no sign of Antonioni in the foyer, and when Atticus asked at the desk he was informed that the great man was in a meeting. A beautiful girl in the hotel's uniform handed him a map of the City.

"Casa Miranda," she said, pointing to a small red dot on the map. "Avere luna bella serata, triste inglese."

"Thank you" said Atticus, catching sight of himself in yet another mirror, apparently understanding Italian. He stood up straight and tried to feel like an attractive Italian man about to meet his lover in a romantic bar in Venice. How hard could it be to find a bar?

Half an hour later, his very British lace-ups were beginning to hurt, and he was decidedly sweaty in his linen jacket. He had followed first one street then another, over countless bridges and across exquisite little squares, until he had no idea where he was, and by the time he passed a particularly rowdy little bar filled with gondoliers in striped jerseys singing what sounded like rugby songs, for the third time, he knew he was hopelessly lost.

He stopped and consulted the incomprehensible map. Lines which looked like streets had turned out to be canals, others were dead ends, or at least blocked by skips of building rubble or bins. Time and again, just as he had been convinced he was a block away, he had found his route cut off by water. He had made his way down streets so dark he had been convinced night had fallen suddenly, before emerging again, into the same little square he had crossed just minutes before. The map would have been of more use, he realised if the streets had carried any sort of signage. Casa Miranda was apparently in in a street named Campiello San Tomà, but as none of the streets had any names on them, it was impossible to work out whether he was miles away or right next to it.

As he stood there, the light fading round him, and people scurrying purposefully past, all knowing exactly where they were going, Atticus's rising anxiety abated for a moment, as he realised just how beautiful his surroundings were. All around him were fabulous crumbling buildings, their high windows lit by the dim lamps favoured by Venetians, people living their lives in this extraordinary city, doing their washing, cooking their dinner, putting their children to bed. At ground level, more brightly lit bars and restaurants were welcoming the early drinkers and diners, forming strings of glittering choices for the tourist and the local alike, centuries of history meeting modern luxury with magical results, only slightly influenced by the ever-present and completely unique smell of the canal water.

Atticus looked hopefully at a group of young people, all in full evening dress, and carrying bottles of champagne, laughing and swaying as they made their way over a bridge towards him but they didn't see him, or if they did they were not inclined to stop. Then he walked over to one of the gondoliers, who was waiting at a table outside the bar but as Atticus got closer, his mate joined him, bearing a tray laden with tankards of beer and with four or five more equally rowdy boatmen in tow.

Atticus was close to despair.

"Oi!" said a bright female voice from across the square. "You alright?"

He looked over to where a pretty redheaded girl in a curiously shiny scarlet dress was standing behind a picnic table on the steps of a small church. On the table were cards, a top hat, and a stuffed white rabbit. As he looked at her, the girl put the rabbit into the hat, put the hat on her head and took it off again with a flourish, to demonstrate that the rabbit had disappeared.

"Poof!" she shouted with glee, and laughed such a delightful laugh that Atticus found that he was laughing too. He went over to her.

"You look lost," said the girl.

"Do I?' said Atticus airily, "Oh no, I was just getting my bearings. Breathing in the atmosphere."

"The stink more like," said the girl. You can't get away from it can you? It's pretty enough here but even I can't magic away the smell of that water, and I'm a magician."

A couple whom Atticus judged to be tourists by their pale faces and nervous smiles approached, and the girl waved a wand over their heads, releasing a little cloud of glitter. Then she performed a series of rapid and very effective card tricks for them, before producing a fresh rose from the man's travel bag and presenting it to his wife. The man, as embarrassed as his wife was enchanted, produced a substantial Euro note and the girl pocketed it neatly as they moved away.

"Wow," said Atticus, forgetting he was supposed to be a seasoned and indifferent traveller. "You're brilliant."

"I am aren't I?" she said, sweeping the cards, the hat, the rabbit and a number of other miscellaneous items Atticus hadn't noticed earlier, into a huge bag which appeared to be fashioned from an eiderdown. "Come on," she said, "You can buy me a drink, and then I'll show you how to get where you're going."

Atticus looked surreptitiously at his watch. He was torn between a definite desire for a drink, especially a drink with this rather splendid girl, and his equally pressing need to get to Casa Miranda. On the other hand, he would almost certainly never be able to do the second of these options, if he didn't go along with the first.

"You've got loads of time," the girl said, as if reading his mind. "Everyone's always really late for everything in Venice. Its practically the law."

Atticus followed the girl down a side street and down a couple of steps into what at first looked like a dingy basement, but once his eyes became accustomed to the limited light, he realised he was in a cosy and extremely crowded bar. Low red lights lit the faces of the customers, and some funky saxophone music could faintly be heard over the general buzz.

"I'm Kate by the way," the girl shouted over her shoulder, using the eiderdown bag to help her barge a way through the throng, "You get a seat, I'll grab the drinks."

Atticus was glad enough to give up trying to follow in the wake of the spirited Kate, but looked in vain for anything which could pass as a seat, until suddenly, by chance, a young couple got up from a corner, and he was able to slip in before anybody noticed. He felt slightly guilty, being in usual circumstances the type of man who believed life was altogether better if people observed queuing and waited their turn, but these were far from usual circumstances. Within an equally surprisingly short time, Kate was on her way back, brandishing a bottle of Prosecco and two huge glasses.

"Well done on the seats," she shouted over the noise, "You must be lucky. Most of the men I know just stand around in bars, and because I'm so little I have to talk to their chests all evening. Mind, you most of my mates complain men only ever address their tits, so I suppose I'm levelling the score."

She dumped the bag on the table between them, spilling feathers and small amounts of coloured talcum powder onto the surface and handed him the bottle. Atticus made a reasonably decent job of opening it, and they each raised a large glass of the pale sparkling wine.

"Cheers!" said Kate, "Here's to new friends."

"Cheers to you," said Atticus, remembering Laura with a slight pang of guilt.

"Don't worry," said Kate, reading his mind again, "I'll have you at your party or whatever it is you're going to, in plenty of time. Where are you going anyway?"

"Um, Casa Miranda," Atticus said, "It's just drinks. Not a party. Although I am here for a party, but that's not until tomorrow night. Tonight I'm meeting someone at Casa Miranda"

"Miranda," said Kate, with an odd look on her face, "Right."

"Do you know it?"

"Oh yes. I know it alright."

"Is it a nice place? A good bar I mean?"

"It's lovely. If you like that kind of thing. Well swanky. You'll love it. Both of you."

"Both of us?"

"It's not the kind of place you go on your own. You and your girlfriend. Wife?"

"How do you know I'm meeting a woman?"

"That jacket, the fact that you keep looking at your watch. Your shoes."

"My shoes? Don't you start. Hilly's always on at me about my shoes. She says shoes are very important in knowing what sort of man a man is. If you see what I mean"

Kate laughed. "She's right there. But I like your shoes, they're very English. And you're obviously not trying to pretend you're Italian, which is a relief. Is Hilly your wife?"

Atticus smiled at the thought of Hilly. He wondered what she would be doing right now. Probably battling laundry and the twins' feeding time, while trying to read a novel for her Book Club, and looking for a cufflink or a pair of matching socks for Hal. And here was he, drinking quite decent wine with a strange and extremely pretty girl he'd only just met in this City of Dreams. Hilly would like Kate, he decided.

"Hilly's my sister. Hermione, but everyone calls her Hilly."

"And you? what does everybody call you?"

"Atticus. Everyone calls me Atticus."

"*Atticus?* God, you do go in for names in your family don't you? What's your mum's name, Boadicea?"

Atticus laughed again. "No, she's Rachel. But my father came from a long line of eccentrically named mad people. He was Columbus, and my grandfather was Eglington."

"Eglington?" Kate spluttered into her wine. "You got off lightly Tix."

"Tix?"

"I shall call you Tix."

Atticus considered it for a moment. "Works for me," he said happily.

Around them, the noise levels rose as more and more people crowded into the bar.

"This is clearly the place to be," said Atticus.

"It's fun. Good vibe. I come here most evenings. If I've got enough for a bottle of this."

Atticus rummaged in his inside pocket. "Sorry," he said, "I should have said. Let me get these."

Kate waved him away, "It's cool," she said, "I've had a good day. Americans. If I couldn't buy a drink for a lost stranger in my town, who would I be?"

"Is it your town?" said Atticus, "You live here?"

"No, I commute from Hertfordshire," Kate laughed. "Joke! Of course I live here. Who wouldn't? Look at it! Its the most utterly fabulous place in the whole world. And the living, is goo-oo-ood!"

She leant back and waved her glass in a silent toast to the whole city. Atticus felt as though he was in a wonderfully romantic film. Fellini. Or given his linen jacket and brogues, probably rather more Richard Curtis. Anyway, something millions of people would go to see in dingy multiplexes on rainy English afternoons, and wish they were him.

"I'll drink to that," he said.

"No," said Kate, suddenly more serious. She leant forward and looked into his eyes with her own pale grey ones. "Let's drink to *us*. Strangers in Paradise."

And equally unexpectedly, she laughed again, her shiny sunset-coloured curls bobbing up and down. "Don't mind me," she said, "I'm a magician."

"You are indeed," Atticus said, almost to himself, "You are indeed."

And then, all too soon, the bottle was empty and Atticus realised the time.

"Oh God!" he said, "It's half past seven! I was supposed to be there at six, and I still don't know where it is!"

Kate seemed oblivious to his sense of urgency.

"Oh you'll be alright," she said, "They'll hardly have got started."

"You know that do you?" said Atticus, sounding crosser than he felt, and in any case, cross only with himself.

"Oh yes," said Kate, gathering her things together in a leisurely fashion.

"So where is it that I'm going?" Atticus said as they struggled out of the bar against the tide of incoming revellers.

"Casa Miranda?" said Kate, "You *really* want to go?"

Atticus found himself standing very close to her in the doorway. He could smell her fresh floral perfume, and breathe in her shiny youthfulness. There were traces of the glitter she used in her act lodged in her hair, and he put out a hand to brush it away before realising what he was doing and putting his hand firmly in a pocket.

"I have to," he said, "I've been invited. I wouldn't even be here if it wasn't for...well, I *have* to."

Kate leant up until she was level with his ear, and whispered.

"It's next door," she said. "Look."

And he looked, and saw the letters 'Casa Miranda' over a fairly ostentatious door just feet away from where they were standing.

"Good heavens. It was here all the time!" he said, turning back. "Thank ......you"

But Kate had vanished.

Chapter Sixteen

Feeling rather alone, Atticus stood in the street outside Casa Miranda for some minutes, trying to prepare himself. The elegant door in front of him gave little away, except for the obvious difference between this establishment and the one he had just left. He pressed a dark brass bell set into the wall and the door opened on an electronic release.

The elegant interior was completely at odds with the outside of the building. This was no Venetian palazzo. It was a sleek modern salon, complete with the ubiquitous mirrors and a lot of white and grey fabric, draped from the ceiling and pooling on the floor, like silent waterfalls.

A few very elegantly dressed people stood around in little groups, speaking in low voices and sipping champagne from ridiculously long flutes. The women wore floor-length dresses in slippery fabrics somewhat at odds with the men who all seemed to be wearing black lounge suits. The whole scene was rather like an advertisement for a very expensive perfume. *Exclusion* by Calvin Klein, Atticus decided.

He stood on the edge of the room, like a spinster at a tea dance, and took one of the long flutes from a tray realising slightly too late that the sculpted figure holding it was actually a real woman sprayed silver with a crown on her head. As he held the rim to his lips, the stem of the glass reached below his waist, and he was sure it was just a matter of time before he forgot it was there and caught it on some passing surface.

He knew he was lucky to be here in what was clearly a very private party, but he couldn't help feeling a bit nostalgic for the cavern next door and the happy company of a magician. This should have been magic, but it wasn't Kate.

"Darling!" he heard across the room, and all thoughts of anything at all were banished. Laura was at his side in a moment. She was wearing a long white dress with a little train which followed her, along with the eyes of everyone else in the room. "You're here at last! I thought you were never coming!"

Atticus felt instantly guilty. "I'm so sorry," he said,"I got er, held up. You know, a call came in and...."

Laura wasn't listening. "Don't you love this place?" she sighed, waving her own long glass, "So chic, so Venice!"

Atticus wasn't at all sure it was either of those things, but he was too stunned by Laura to respond. She chatted away, telling him who everybody was, "That's Massimo, he owns the sweetest gallery in Accademia, and his wife. The one in the emerald Armani? that's Signora Castiletti, owns a palazzo in Murano, you must try and get to one of her soirees while you're here, and of course that's Ranaldini, the great tenor, we're so lucky he's promised to sing for us tomorrow evening, and he never does that for anybody. Probably misses La Fenice, he was always there....."

As she spoke, Atticus watched her, unable to work out exactly what was bothering him about her this evening. Was her voice just a touch too light, her eyes a little too glittery? Her hand shook as she indicated the guests, but that might just have been the weight of the ridiculous champagne glass.

Eventually, her voice drifted into silence, her social duty done, and she turned to face Atticus. "I'm so glad you're here," she said, suddenly, "You know, I think you're my only friend."

Stunned, Atticus was about to protest, when he heard another familiar voice.

" Laura? Carissima?"

The oily but unmistakeable tones of Boran echoed round the room. "You are neglecting our other guests."

Our other guests? Atticus was dreadfully confused. Boran, in a thin black polo-necked sweater, and skinny black jeans which would have looked a bit risky on anyone, but certainly did so on someone his age, had appeared at Laura's side. taking her arm in what looked suspiciously like a tight grip.

"You remember Atticus?" Laura said, rather desperately.

"I don't think so," said Boran.

"No, no, and why indeed should you?" said Atticus cheerily, putting out a hand. "We did meet a couple of weeks ago. At a party. In London. But I expect you meet a lot of people. In your line of work."

"My line of work?"

"Of course I don't actually know what your line of work is," said Atticus hastily, "you didn't mention it, I wonder, what is it in fact, that you do...?" his voice faded, and Laura looked directly at him, her eyebrows raised.

"Anyway, it's been perfectly lovely to see you again," he finished, withdrawing the unshaken hand.

"Laura?" said Boran again, as if Atticus hadn't spoken at all, "The sultan and his wife are anxious to continue our discussion."

He indicated an ominous looking gentleman in long robes standing by a huge palm.

"Absolutely," said Atticus. "I mustn't keep you from a Sultan. I have to go anyway. You know, places to go, people to see..."

He drained the long glass, almost hitting Laura on the chin with the foot of it, as he raised it to his lips.

"I'll just see Atticus out," said Laura quickly, taking the glass and placing it on another silver-sprayed waitress's outstretched hand.

Boran frowned, his heavy eyebrows meeting completely in the middle of his dark forehead. "A moment," he said ominously, "I will wait for you here."

Laura steered Atticus to the door. "It's probably better if you go," she said, "I didn't think - he's not usually like this - He just gets a bit anxious sometimes."

"Laura," said Atticus "I can't help wondering, I mean I'd understand perfectly if....is Boran, your, well, your *boyfriend*? It's just that he seems very keen not to let you out of his sight, and indeed, why would he? I certainly wouldn't if I was...well, I perfectly understand. I mean why would you want to bother with a rather scruffy Englishman without a pair of loafers to his name, when you could be with someone so...so impressive?"

"Boyfriend? Oh no," said Laura, looking at him. "Oh no. Nothing like that. I can't really explain." Suddenly her face softened, and she placed a hand on his sleeve. "Look", she said quietly. "Why don't I pop over to the Campanile Grande later? I could come up to your room, we could have champagne together, a proper chat. How about that?"

"Wow," said Atticus. "Well yes. That would be...Absolutely. You'd be very welcome."

Laura kissed him very lightly on the cheek. He smelt her distinctive Marc Jacobs scent and was ridiculously glad about the present still sitting on his bedside table. He would give it to her later, as the moonlight slanted into his room, with the canal flowing quietly past the window.

"Arrivederci," she said, and never had a casual foreign phrase, used so often in jest by would-be-sexy English people, sounded so genuinely promising.

The trouble was, he hadn't really got any idea of how much later, 'later' would be.

Chapter Seventeen

Atticus returned to his hotel room, his head sightly fizzing from the Prosecco and the champagne, and the lack of food. He thought about ordering room service, but the possibility of Laura arriving just as he was about to tuck into a juicy burger or a basket of chicken and chips was unthinkable. Or worse, the idea of her having to step over a discarded tray outside the door, the train of her dress sweeping the last of the ketchup along behind her.

He ordered a bottle of champagne from the room service menu, and on impulse added some smoked salmon sandwiches. When they arrived, he asked Marco to leave the champagne unopened, and the silver cover over the sandwiches. From time to time as he paced up and down in the huge empty silent room, he heard the light crack of melting ice, as the champagne settled further down into its bucket.

He tried to read, but found he was unable to concentrate, flicking idly through the many glossy magazines which had been placed in the room, pictures of handbags and watches no match for the beauty of the view over the Grand Canal. On the side of a campanile in the distance was a huge wrought iron clock whose hands turned slowly round past ten, and then eleven. The crowds began to drift away from the streets and boats below, and eventually he had to admit that it looked as though Laura wasn't coming.

Of course she wasn't. He had been foolish to think that she would. She had much better things to do, much more important people to be seen with. Even now she was probably dining in some wonderful canalside restaurant with the Sultan and Boran, eating oysters and artichokes, the reflections of a thousand candles flickering in her eyes.

On impulse he picked up his phone,

"Good heavens," said Hilly "Where are you phoning from? It's the middle of the night! Why aren't you out wondering the bohemian streets or exploring the catacombs, or eating spaghetti vongole with the lovely Laura?"

"It's a long story," said Atticus gloomily, "But I can assure you I am entirely alone."

"What a waste of that beautiful room. Loved the picture you sent. I can't imagine what it's costing her. Still never mind, I bet the mini bar's great. And the huge bath, and the lovely soft bed and, well, that's my fantasy, are you having a nice time?"

"I'm not actually sure," said Atticus. "Venice isn't quite what I expected. What's going on your end? It sounds suspiciously quiet."

"Hal's gone to Casualty with Bill again," said Hilly, "Nothing serious, but it probably needs a stitch. I"m here with Ben and she's currently asleep on a pile of laundry which is lying on the kitchen floor waiting to be put into the machine. I have a large glass of Macon Village, and am savouring the moment. Don't think for one minute I want to be in a five-star hotel bed with an enormous duvet and gondoliers serenading me from under my window. Have you seen Bill Nighy yet?"

Atticus laughed. "Sorry, no," he said, "But I'll be sure to look out for him. Give Hal and the twins my love, won't you? Tell them I miss them."

"No you don't. You're in Venice. Atticus, have you actually seen Laura yet?"

"Oh yes, I bumped into her in a bar earlier. But the party's tomorrow night, so I expect we'll have more time together then."

"Right. Of course you will."said Hilly.

"You sound tired." said Atticus.

"Of course I do," said Hilly, "I haven't slept for three and a half years." There was an odd sound like a door being shut and a muffled whisper he couldn't quite catch. Hal must be back from the hospital.

"Look Bro, I have to go...I think, well.. I just need to go. Have fun! Bye!"

And Hilly rang off, but not before Atticus heard what sounded very suspiciously like a man's voice in the background. It was probably the television. Yes, that was it, Hilly was probably watching television.

His own room fell silent again, and the shadows cast across the water by the lights in the streets, reflected on the ceiling. He sat and watched as the light changed slowly from deep deep darkness, to the strange grey light of the pre-dawn, waiting for Laura, who never came, and at about four am, he fell asleep in the big silk lined chair and dreamed of cellos and champagne and mermaids.

Chapter Eighteen

"I'm sorry Hils, I didn't realise you were on the phone."

Graham handed Hilly a drink and took his seat opposite her at the family's dining room table, moving wax crayons, a small green wellington and half an apple pock-marked with the evidence of tiny teeth aside as he did so.

"It's alright, I don't think he heard you." Hilly said slightly shakily. "This is awful. I feel terrible going behind Atticus's back like this."

"I know. But you did the right thing. It's always best to check these things out. Anyway, he's your brother. What are sisters for, if not to look out for a mere man who's lost his way? I wish I had a sister like you."

They looked at each other for a moment, leaving unsaid, the additional statement that he would prefer to have a wife like Hilly.

"And I'm lying to Hal too, and that's even worse!" protested Hilly.

Graham opened the bottle of claret he had brought and poured them each a glass.

"He doesn't know I'm here?"

"No! I was going to tell him you'd called and that you had said you needed to see me, face to face, but then Bill got injured and Hal just picked her up and dashed off to A&E. And even when he phoned later to tell me everything was fine and they were just waiting for a stitch and a plaster, I could hardly tell him that another man arrived at the house within fifteen minutes of his leaving. Could I?"

"When will he be back?"

"It sounds like he'll be another couple of hours at least."

"I'll be on my way before that. Then you won't have to tell him. If you don't want to."

"Of course I'll tell him. What *shall* I tell him?"

"That you asked me, an old colleague and I hope a good friend, for help because you were worried about your brother, and I looked into a couple of things and now I'm here because I've found something I think you should know about, and because now I've opened this particular can of worms there are a few things you might be able to help me with."

"That sounds very serious."

"Well it may be, and it may not be."

Hilly started on her wine. It was almost midnight. Three-year old Ben, oblivious of the drama her twin, her mother and her uncle were caught up in, was still soundly asleep on the kitchen floor.

"You'd better tell me everything." Hilly said.

Chapter Nineteen

Atticus was woken by a sharp knock on the door. Easing himself upright, he realised he had been asleep in the chair for two hours. Below the window the day was already well under way. The refuse barges had hauled away their cargoes of rotting garbage, and made way for the vaporetti and gondolas which were already doing a brisk trade, eager tourists snapping away on their mobile phones and settling into chairs outside street cafes. The working residents of Venice had been at work for some time now, filling their days as everybody did, with decision making, and meetings, and filing and typing, and designing and so on, just as if they weren't sitting in the middle of a lagoon surrounded by staggeringly beautiful crumbling architecture, and seeping black waters, and centuries of history.

He opened the door of the room and a uniformed waiter wheeled a trolley into the room.

"I didn't order anything," said Atticus, acutely aware of the undrunk champagne now wallowing in a bucket of tepid water, and the sandwiches, almost certainly dried and curled in their silver cave. He might as well have had a sign on his head reading 'disappointed lover' He was pretty sure the waiter was finding it amusing.

"I'll have the champagne later," he said brusquely, "you might send up some more ice."

The waiter nodded and backed away, without even trying for a tip. The tale he had to tell of the poor lonely man in the Andante Suite was worth far more than a handful of small change. Atticus took the cloth off the trolley and saw a supremely pretty breakfast laid out, croissants, jam, butter, a little plate of wafer-thin Italian cold meats, a dish of fresh fruit, including blueberries, his absolute favourite, a silver jug of what smelt like excellent coffee, and a large white envelope with his name written on it.

He realised he was incredibly hungry, and forked a decent bundle of the cold meat into his mouth before opening the envelope. The smoky, piggy taste of the ham filled his head, and as he stood there, still in his clothes, eating the proper Italian breakfast, with the Grand Canal flowing by and some very good looking correspondence to deal with, he cheered up considerably, feeling as much like a true Continental traveller as it was possible to feel.

The envelope yielded up an invitation so stiff he could have used it to scrape ice off windscreens. Gold-embossed and with gold edging it was, dare he even think it - a bit over the top, but hell, this was Venice and this was a party invitation. *The* party invitation. The address was that of a private palazzo, a quick look at the hopeless map suggested it was on the edge of the city. Apparently a water taxi would arrive to collect him at seven for cocktails, then dinner and dancing. And the dress code was black tie. Atticus sent up a silent Thank you to Hilly for suggesting he bring his dinner jacket, and to Great Uncle Horatio for the trust fund which had bought it, made-to-measure from Savile Row, and had freed him from a lifetime of hired dinner jackets smelling of dry cleaning fluid, cigarette smoke, and disappointed men.

God this was exciting. Maybe it was the lack of proper sleep, or the intense flavours of the breakfast, the deep buttery croissants, and brilliance of the morning light off the Canal, or the promise of Laura and the Palazzo, or maybe it was a combination of all of them, but Atticus had started to enjoy himself. Really properly enjoy himself.

He kicked off his shoes, threw off his clothes and put on the hotel robe which hung on the back of the bathroom door. No scratchy thick towelling for the *Campanile Grande*, the robe was floor length, with a fine cotton weave lining and a luxurious silk outer layer which flowed around him and made him feel like Noel Coward. He admired himself in the mirror, before taking a second croissant over to the bed where he planned to sit for a moment, before having a marvellous bath.

And then it was ten o clock and another knock on the door woke him. He sat up suddenly, covered in butter and croissant, his fingers sticky with jam, and the coffee stone cold, still in its jug.

He wrapped the robe tightly round him and went to the door. He couldn't possibly be expecting any more room service. Perhaps it was Laura. He *knew* it was Laura. He didn't have time to get dressed, and he suspected he could do with a shower. His hair was sticking up on one side, as it always did when he had slept heavily.

"Who is it?" he said through the door.

There was no answer. It *was* Laura. She would never stoop to shouting through a hotel room keyhole. There was nothing for it. He threw open the door. "Laura, sweetheart," he said, "you're here at last!"

"Ah," said a voice which was very definitely not Laura's, "You're expecting someone else."

"Kate!" said Atticus. "Wow! You're , how did you find me? I... er, no, I wasn't exactly expecting someone else...it's great to see you!"

"Well whether you were or whether you weren't, you might want to rethink that robe," said Kate, stepping into the room. "Seriously deadly. Wow! Some gaff. Gorgeous."

She did a quick tour of the suite checking out the bathroom, running her little hands over the fine furniture, and stopping as everyone must surely do, to admire the spectacular view. "You must be someone very important."

"Oh no," Atticus ran a hand through his hair. "I'm really not anyone."

Kate had uncovered the smoked salmon sandwiches. "These seem to have been here for a while. May I?" and she took one over to the window. "I'm always hungry."

"Kate, it's lovely to see you," said Atticus sincerely.

"I thought I might show you my town," said Kate, "if you're not too busy with, what did you say her name was, Laura? Was she the one you were meeting last night, or have you picked up a rival magician on the steps of another basilica?"

Atticus laughed. "There could never be another to rival you," he said, "And yes, Laura is the one I was meeting, although I didn't actually get to spend any time with her as she was very busy. I thought she might have popped round to catch up this morning, but..." and here he looked round the vast suite, "it seems she is still busy."

"Oops," said Kate, "do I detect the whiff of unrequited love?"

"Of course not," said Atticus. "Look, I'd love to come out with you. Just give me ten minutes to grab a shower and a clean shirt, and we'll go. Help yourself to sandwiches."

And just less than the suggested ten minutes later, they stepped out of the hotel into the bright sunshine, Atticus still slightly damp from his shower, and Kate, still carrying the voluminous eiderdown bag, into which she had put the last of the sandwiches and a small ashtray with the hotel's logo on it.

"Now where shall we start?" she mused, "This way!"

Chapter Twenty

Venice was extraordinary, thought Atticus as he followed Kate through the tiny streets. With every turn he came upon new treasures. The City seemed to be made up of tiny villages, some characterised by high dark buildings which almost seemed to meet at the top, shutting out all but the tiniest line of sky, whilst round another corner he found a little square with pale pink houses all round it, green shutters thrown wide and lines of washing joining them at head height. Then there were the churches, the grand ornate Basilicas bearing down like disapproving ancestors, and the little wooden ones, with their doors open spilling out black-clad great-aunts with baskets of bread or flowers.

Every few minutes, they went over a bridge, some small stone affairs, under which small wooden boats paddled, others wider and grander, with gondolieri deftly manoeuvring their craft underneath.

Kate seemed to know exactly where she was going. Today she was wearing a long velvet coat, in bright green, faded on the shoulders and darker at the hem, where it hung down and almost brushed the cobbled streets. The fading of the colour made her look almost as though she was rising out of the water herself, yet Kate was a great deal more human than any mermaid. Occasionally she would wave at a passing boatman, or shout a cheerful greeting to a shop owner standing in a doorway. The ubiquitous eiderdown bag bulged, yet she seemed not to find it heavy at all, which was a relief, as Atticus might have felt he should offer to carry it.

Eventually, after what seemed like hours but was in fact just a few minutes, they came out of a dark side street and the world opened up before them. An enormous cloud of pigeons took to the air, with a mighty flapping of wings, and Kate laughed, turning to him.

"Look," she cried, "Look! the most wonderful sight in the whole world!"

So this was St Mark's Square, thought Atticus, staring up at the magnificent buildings, the cloistered edges where the exclusive shops mixed with tourist emporia on two sides, and the row of gilded cafes and bars on the third side, where the hundreds of tables were already busy with morning trade, and aproned waiters bore aloft trays of coffee and pastries and Prosecco.

And over all this, presided the great Basilica of San Marco, the Doge's apartments and the campanile, the iconic sights that anyone who has ever heard of Venice or even done a jigsaw puzzle, would know in an instant.

It was always odd, being close to something with which one was so familiar, and yet which one has never actually seen, reflected Atticus, not for the first time. It looks exactly as you think it should, and yet it *feels,* completely different.

"Florian's of course!" shouted Kate, from halfway across the square.

As he approached the world-famous tables outside Florian's cafe, Atticus couldn't see any spare tables. He was disappointed. After all, this was one of the things you just had to do if you were in Venice. Maybe they would have to order at the bar, drink their coffee standing, as the Italians did, although to be fair, few Italians had coffee at Florian's at all, preferring the cheaper little bars in the alleyways where coffee was no doubt far better, and certainly cheaper, but less romantic.

The next moment, he realised Kate had secured a table, and a slightly disconsolate couple in matching outward-bound cagoules were heading away, having been told that the seats they had their eyes on were reserved '*por la signora bellissima*'.

"Thanks Harvey," said Kate, and the waiter bent to kiss her on both cheeks.

"For you angel, anything," he said in a voice that was decidedly British Midlands, "the usual for you?"

"And my friend," said Kate, "Harve - this is Atticus. He's *so* one of us. Tix, meet Harve, he's from Solihull."

Atticus put out a hand, and Harvey shook it very firmly. "I know who you are," he said, with a hint of menace, staring Atticus in the eye.

"I'm sorry," said Atticus, "I don't think...."

"Any mate of Katie's" said Harvey. "As long as you *are* a mate of Katie's."

"Well," said Kate, apparently not noticing the exchange, "where else could we possibly start if not Florians? Now, we have a lot to do, so we can't linger. But you have to try the special."

Harvey was gone less than a minute and returned with two tiny cups of espresso, two long flutes of Prosecco, a small glass of what looked like dark yellow wine, and a plate of fluffy golden bread with raisins in it.

"Panettone," said Kate, taking the yellow wine and pouring it lightly over the bread. "Here. You'll love it."

She put a forkful into Atticus's open mouth, and he did indeed love it. What he also loved was the sudden awareness that, to the rest of the world, he was sitting in one of its most beautiful places, with a pretty girl feeding him cakes and wine, and looking like a man in love.

In love? A pigeon, sitting on the next table looking hopefully at the panettone put its head on one side and looked at him quizzically. Get a grip man, who do you think you are? it seemed to say.

Suddenly, Kate grabbed Atticus's phone, and leaning in towards him, she took a picture of them both. The Florian's sign was in the background.

"There," she said, "A proper Selfie. Now you can show everybody we were here. Send it to your sister. She'll be thrilled!"

Atticus wasn't sure he wanted to send Hilly a picture in which he appeared to be with someone who wasn't the someone he was supposed to be with. But he didn't like to refuse Kate, so after a moment's hesitation, he opened up a message box under the picture.

Me with a friend, having a quick coffee! x

Behind them, just inside the door of Florian's, a young man in white tie and tails sat at the grand piano and began to play. Harvey, passing between the tables with a laden tray said over his shoulder to

Kate, "That's Dippo. Plays in a heavy metal band over in Mestre weekends. You'd never think it would you? Bit of a git but he brings the tips in."

But Atticus barely heard Harvey's remark, because a few tables away, behind a copy of *Corriere Della Sera,* and with a sizeable glass of beer in front of him, was Yellowhair. Atticus looked again, but he was sure. It was definitely him. He'd know that jacket-and-jumper combo anywhere.

"What?" said Kate, noticing, "you look as though you've seen a ghost."

"No," said Atticus. "Not a ghost. Just that man. I've seen him before. In fact I've seen him quite a lot. Do you know him?"

"Which one?" Kate looked over, but Yellowhair had gone. Harvey was by the table, collecting the folded newspaper and the empty beer glass. He gave Atticus a long, and possibly significant look.

"Well he certainly seems to have something more important to do, whoever he is," Kate said, "and so do we. Come on!"

"I should pay," said Atticus, "Have you got the bill?"

Kate laughed. "We don't pay," she said. "I never pay."

Harvey waved as they left, so obviously the not-paying thing wasn't a problem, at least for him.

Chapter Twenty-One

They continued their journey through the streets, Kate occasionally pointing out small things that anyone unfamiliar with the city would miss, a beautiful doorway, a pretty window box, a view from a particular corner. He saw bakeries tucked inside houses, and potters and painters working away in dark doorways. There were narrow shops tucked away, where cheery shopowners sold fruit and ornaments and flowers wrapped in bright paper, and the wonderful *cartoleria*, where all manner of beautiful stationery was laid out, alongside hand-tooled leather journals which begged to have poetry written in them, and fountain pens made of glass, with bottles of ink in all the colour of the rainbow.

"Right," said Kate, coming to a stop outside a tiny shop by the side of a small bridge. "This is a must."

The shop window was almost hidden by a cloud of feathers, gilt paper, and sequins, but Kate found a small door, and as they went in, Atticus felt as though he was stepping into a tiny bird house, filled with exotic creatures. His eyes slowly accustomed to the limited light, and he realised he was looking at masks, hundreds and hundreds of them, some on shelves, some standing on sticks in jars and vases, some pinned to the ceiling. Eyes seemed to follow him round the room, although of course eyes were the one thing the masks didn't have.

"Isn't this fun?" said Kate. "Now you choose. One for you and one for me."

And then she disappeared into the back of the shop.

Atticus amused himself for a while, playing about with the various masks, and having discovered a small mirror, tried on several options, before settling on a black sequinned affair with a white ostrich feather trim and an elegant silver chain to attach it to a costume. There was still no sign of Kate, so he carried on looking, weighing up the choice between a pink and gold princess mask, and a brilliantly-coloured Harlequin affair.

Eventually she reappeared, busying herself with the eiderdown bag. She seemed satisfied with whatever she had been doing, saying over her shoulder "lasciare a me, ci vediamo presto," to someone behind her. It sounded like music to Atticus.

"Perfect," she said, looking at the two masks in Atticus's hands, "I love them both. Which have you chosen? And as he held the black mask over his own face, she laughed. "Very mysterious. Well done!" and she put his mask, and the Harlequin into the eiderdown bag.

They didn't pay.

"Arrivederci amigo!" she called over her shoulder as they left.

"Now lunch," she said firmly, "It's not far."

And indeed it wasn't. Two bridges, two left turns and a right, past a woman selling the most heavenly scented roses in a dark doorway, and they were standing outside a jolly-looking trattoria. One glance inside told Atticus this was a place where local people ate lunch. It was as full of men in striped jerseys, beribboned hats and deck shoes as an amateur dramatic society production of *The Gondoliers*.

"I know," said Kate, following Atticus's gaze, "But they're fun. Think of them like London's black cabbies. They're a sort of secret society, but they can always be relied upon to get you out of trouble. You'll see."

Atticus hadn't imagined he would be in any trouble. They went in, where yet again, Kate was greeted as an old friend, and they were shown to two impossibly high stools at one end of the bar. It was unfair on the shorter man, Atticus thought to install these stools. It made one look so daft, feet swinging inches off the floor, and the tendency to swivel round when one least expected it, leaving you staring out into the room, while your lunch companion talked to the back of your head.

"Look Kate," he began, "Before we order anything. I have to insist on buying you lunch. You haven't let me pay for anything yet, and I really have to insist."

"Wow," said Kate after a moment. "You insisting. Masterful. But before you get all American Express on me, let me show you something."

She slid off her barstool, nodded to the maitre-d' who saluted her, and taking her bag, moved into the centre of the room. Rapping on the table with a long handled spoon, she put on the Harlequin mask. Then, gathering up the skirt of her long coat, she got up on a chair, and produced two pretty white doves from the depths of the eiderdown bag. The same eiderdown bag which Atticus had had in his sight for several hours. And which most certainly had not had any livestock in it earlier.

A cloud of glitter wafted across the room as Kate waved one arm and then the other over the heads of the gondoliers tucking into their pizza, and a frankly frightened looking couple who had wandered in by accident.

Then she took a glass from one of the gondoliers, drained it of the last of the red wine he was drinking and threw it into the air. Fearing a crash, everybody waited, breath held. There was no crash. The glass had disappeared. There was a round of applause. Several people who had been studying the menu from outside the restaurant came in to see what was going on, and enchanted by the sight, took seats at tables. The maitre d signified his thanks to Kate, as she got down from the chair and returned to Atticus.

"That's why we don't pay here either," she said. "Now what shall we have?"

Atticus was so busy studying the enormous menu, that he was only vaguely aware of another diner as he entered the bar and took a seat right at the other end. Suddenly, like two cowboys in a western, the two men looked straight at each other along the full length of the zinc bar top. It was Boran.

"Don't bother with the menu," said Kate. "It's all good." She hit Atticus lightly over the head with the card, and another cloud of pink glitter floated over his head. The barman laughed. By the time Atticus opened his eyes again, Boran had disappeared, and a neat plate of the most delicious smelling fettuccine had appeared, alongside a glass of red wine. He had probably imagined Boran. What would he be doing in a place like this?

"So," said Kate, as they began their lunch which was as excellent as it promised to be. "Tell me about her."

"About who?" said Atticus through pasta.

"About this Laura. The one you love."

"Laura?" To tell the truth, Atticus had temporarily forgotten about Laura. How had he done that? Laura, the most wonderful, amazing incredible woman, who had wonderfully, amazingly, incredibly chosen him, to be her date at a party in Venice? Who had sent him an upgraded plane ticket and a reservation at one of Venice's most expensive and exclusive hotels because she loved him? And within just hours of arriving, here he was, having breakfast, and lunch, and magic and masks bestowed upon him by another woman? Even for a seasoned Lothario this would be fast work, and Atticus was no Lothario. After, well, after what happened last year with Flora, he hadn't so much as looked at a woman, beautiful or otherwise, and now, one sniff of an exotic location and he was acting as though he was Gerard Butler.

"Laura," he said eventually. "Well, as it happens I was at school with her."

"She's quite old then," said Kate.

"Old? Atticus pictured Laura, this time, oddly in school uniform. That didn't work at all. Had she ever worn the uniform? She must have done. The school had been very hot on that sort of thing. So it was odd that he couldn't remember Laura in it. "She's not, I mean I'm not...."

Kate was laughing. "Go on," she said.

"She looked me up. Asked me to a party in London," Atticus explained. And suddenly, he remembered where he had seen Yellowhair before. He re-ran his memory of the second-floor landing of that house in Mayfair in his head, and saw him, quite distinctly, standing at the top of the stairs. With the man in glasses who had been so busily avoiding Atticus's eye at the airport. They had both been at the party. And they had both been at the airport. And now, Yellowhair at least, was here.

"Hey! come back to me dreamer," said Kate, putting her hand gently on the side of his face. "I've never been to a party that did *that* to me!"

"Sorry," said Atticus. "I was just....Anyway, then she sent me an invitation to this party. Here, in Venice. And it's tonight."

"Wow," said Kate, "And you like her enough to spend all this money on coming here, and a posh hotel and all that?"

Atticus thought for a minute. He couldn't possibly tell her that he'd let another woman pay his way. It was beginning to look like a habit. "I suppose I must do," he said, and felt dreadful. Lying didn't come naturally.

"Liar," said Kate.

"What?" Atticus couldn't believe he had been found out so soon.

"There's no *suppose so* about it. You're besotted. Is she very beautiful?"

This was easier. "Yes, she is," said Atticus, truthfully.

"Lucky her," said Kate, adding, "To be beautiful." Lest he should think for one minute that she thought Laura was lucky to have Atticus.

"Does your sister, Hermia?..."

"Hilly."

"Hilly. Does she approve? You seem very close."

"Hilly was at school with Laura too of course. We were at the same school. All of us. Although Hilly doesn't remember....that is, she hasn't really....said."

Atticus realised it was true. He had no idea what Hilly thought, because she hadn't really said. Which was very unlike her. Hilly was someone who usually lost no time in *saying*.

"Affogato," said Kate, as the waiter cleared away the pasta plates.

"Affogato," said Atticus, politely. Kate laughed again.

"No, silly, 'Grazie' means Thank you. Affogato is a dessert. Which we are very much having."

"How did you know I thought Affogato meant Thank you?"

"I always know what you're thinking," said Kate.

"So," she said a while later, as they emerged blinking from the restaurant, warm with wine and good food and amaretto liqueur, the staff waving and cheering them as though they were famous, "We should go shopping. Shopping is good here. You must need something."

Atticus thought. "Not really," he said, "Although now you mention it, I still don't have any loafers."

"You really are obsessed with shoes aren't you? But you definitely want loafers?"

"I don't know. But everyone else seems to have them. I just have these." Atticus indicated his rather worn brown lace-ups, "and my black dress shoes for wearing with my dinner jacket. And I have slippers obviously. At home."

"Of course you do."

"I was in a shop at the airport, buying, well.. never mind what I was buying, and the chaps in there said I should go somewhere called Cassini? I wrote it down somewhere," Atticus fished about in his jacket for the scrap of paper he had written the address on.

"Rue d'Ivola," said Kate. "Yes, I suppose if I was to buy loafers, in another life possibly, I would probably go to Cassini. Come on."

And she led the way through more of the cobbled labyrinth that was Venice, with the afternoon shadows moving across their way and a sleepiness pervading the streets, until they found themselves in an altogether more upmarket district, lined with luxury goods shops and designer label boutiques.

"Rue d-Ivola," said Kate, "I hope your wallet's up to it."

At first glance, the shop, like those all the way along this beautiful street, appeared to be more like an art gallery. The walls were brilliant white, and huge spotlights bounced off the walls directing pools of almost blinding intensity onto small specks of colour as though a child had dropped a box of paints on a clean tiled floor. However on closer inspection, the pockets of colour turned out to be shoes. Loafers in fact, beautifully lined up in pairs around the room in every colour imaginable. A single pair of powder-blue suede ones, complete with white tassels, sat in the centre of the window.

As they stood looking in at the shoes, two extremely thin Italian men entered the shop, and began ordering a rather harassed assistant about. As he ran round them, proffering box after box of the shoes, and the two men paraded up and down in them, Atticus regretted mentioning the loafers in the first place.

"Are they very expensive?" he asked. There was no price on the shoes in the window.

"I'll go and ask," said Kate, and before he could stop her, she had flung open the door and gone in.

Atticus could only watch in dismay as Kate and the assistant conversed with a great deal of dramatic hand signals, while the two customers looked more and more enraged. Eventually Kate spoke directly to the Italians, and then, after even more expansive gesturing, she came out of the shop.

"Goodness!" said Atticus, "Are you alright? What was that all about?"

"Oh I was just asking Jerome how his cello practice was coming along," she said, "He's very good you know, quite talented I'm told, but he's very bad at practising. His mum despairs. She says he'll never be any better than a shoe shop assistant if he carries on this way. Seven hundred by the way."

"Seven hundred?"

"Quid. For the shoes in the window. The others are all roughly the same price."

The two Italians were waving credit cards about, and Jerome was busily boxing shoes.

"They seem happy enough."

"Two pairs each. I told them there was a discount for two. They live in Milan. Nob heads."

Atticus laughed. "Am I a nob-head?"

Only if you're prepared to pay seven hundred pounds for ice-cream-coloured shoes."

She took his arm and they turned away. As they headed down the street she asked:

"What colour would you have chosen, if you had been going to buy loafers?"

"Brown I expect," said Atticus.

"That's alright then," she said, cheerfully. "Now, talking of ice cream...."

Chapter Twenty-Two

"The thing is, I think I may have been worrying unnecessarily." Hilly was speaking into the phone in a low voice, aware that Hal was upstairs. She was half listening to the sound of the shower, knowing she was fine as long as she could hear it.

"Well that sounds like good news, what makes you think that?" Graham sounded surprised.

"After you left last night, I couldn't sleep, not that there's anything new about that obviously. But I kept going over and over what you'd told me, in my head. Do you know I even thought about telling Hal everything and asking him to hold the fort while I go over to Venice and try to rescue Atticus?"

"Well, I would have stopped you. If I'm right, that would be very dangerous."

"But that's just it. I think you may not be right. I mean, you might be, but it might not matter. To me, to us. Of course it *matters*, it matters to you, that's your job. But it might not be an issue for Atticus."

"How so?"

"Well the thing is, as you know, I was convinced he was completely besotted with this girl, and with what happened last year, with Flora, and the fact that he hasn't shown so much as a whiff of interest in anyone else, even though I introduced him to some of my loveliest friends. I was worried when he seemed to be taking Laura Hutchinson so seriously. Especially when she started throwing all her money about. He was such a sitting target, a lonely chap with not enough to do, no job, and feeling like an absolute shit because of what happened with Flora, believing he wasn't worthy of anyone's love, let alone the attention and frankly showy-off bank balance of the supposedly fabulous Laura."

"Quite. From what I understand, it is quite possible he may have overestimated her romantic interest."

"But then Hal came home with Bill, and we put the twins to bed, and then after Hal had talked me through every step of the A&E experience..."

"No permanent damage I hope?"

"No, just a tiny stitch under the hairline, and a few bruises, and lots of advice as to how to keep children occupied and out of trouble. Ha! They obviously don't have any *idea* what life is like in our house. Anyway, Hal and I were both so tired that we sort of fell asleep ourselves, on the sofa, and when I woke up, there was a text from Atticus, with a picture of him at Florian's in St Mark's Square..."

"Nice. Very romantic. Ever been?"

"Of course not. Hal would point out that the coffee was far better standing at some tin bar in an alleyway accompanied by chain-smoking fishermen."

"Pity" Graham was imagining sharing Prosecco and Espresso at Florian's with Hilly.

"But the thing is, he was with someone else entirely!"

"Someone else?"

"Yup. Another girl. Pretty, one of those fun sorts, with mad red hair and a velvet coat thing that I would wear if only you could get porridge out of velvet. They looked *happy*."

"So, let me get this straight. He's gone to Venice, on an all-expenses luxury break, paid for by this Laura, and now he's having tea and buns with someone else. Is that it?"

"Absolutely. And I couldn't be more relieved. He obviously isn't besotted with Laura Hutchinson at all. In fact, he hasn't mentioned her."

"Isn't he supposed to be going to some sort of party with her?"

"Officially yes. This evening I think. Perhaps he'll take this other girl."

"Not terribly good manners in the circumstances."

"You're right." Hilly thought for a moment. "That wouldn't do at all, would it. Perhaps he'll skip the party?"

"Worse."

"What would Ma do? She would go to the party, talk to everybody, make sure everyone had seen and heard her, and then leave, hoping nobody would notice. That's what he'll do! And then he can spend a lovely romantic evening in a candlelit bar with this new girl, and they'll plan when they can come and see me, and we can all get to know each other."

"Hang on a minute. He's in Venice, she's in Venice. She's probably Italian!"

"No, No. She doesn't look Italian at all. She's English. I'd bet on it."

Graham laughed."You're always so certain about detail Hils, it's one of the things I love about you. But sometimes,you're so focussed on the certainties, as you see them, that you fail to see the bigger picture. It's entirely possible, never mind probable, this girl is Italian. And if she isn't, it's equally likely that she's American. Or German or Dutch."

"Dutch? I've never met anyone Dutch."

"And it's highly likely you won't meet this one. Heidi, as we shall now call her, as we don't know her name..."

"Heidi was Swiss."

"Detail again. Anika then. She's probably just another tourist, seeing a poor lonely man hanging about in Venice, and decided to send a selfie to her mates."

"On *his* phone."

"Why not? perhaps she doesn't have one."

"Everyone has a phone."

"Look dear one, I'm thrilled you think Atticus isn't in as much danger as we thought, and I'm very *very* glad you aren't dropping everything to dash over there and get mixed up in anything..."

"Who says there's anything to get mixed up in? You said last night that it was just *possible* that..."

"Possible, yes."

Hilly realised the noise of the shower upstairs had stopped.

"Look I'll have to go. Just thought I should let you know we're out of danger. Just me being over protective as usual."

"Another of your most endearing traits."

"I'm not sure Hal would agree."

"I really should meet Hal one day. If I'm to admit defeat I may as well do it gracefully and to the face of the man who has dashed my dreams."

"Graham, you are so lovely. Thank you, *Thank you!*"

Hilly turned her phone off, and put it in her pocket. But not before Hal, emerging from the kind of violent power shower you have to have if you've spent half the night in Casualty and the other half on a sofa, came into the kitchen, and overheard his wife's last remark.

"Who was that?" he asked, as they both went into the kitchen and began clearing a pathway through toys and discarded clothes and sprayed breakfast cereal to get to the kettle.

"Oh. Just one of the girls from the nursery," Hilly said lightly, "Apparently Ben spilled the beans about last night's accident and they were worried about whether they should be looking for symptoms of concussion or anything."

Hal filled the kettle, looking out into the garden. Surely it wasn't possible Hilly was lying to him. Hilly never lied to anyone about anything. But he was sure, absolutely sure, that she had heard her say 'Graham'. There was nobody at the nursery called Graham. He should know, he did the nursery drop-off at least as often as Hilly did, and the lovely, but young girls who ran Little Pilgrims were always more than happy to have him help out with moving furniture, unblocking sinks full of poster paint and putting up paper chains.

"Right," he said, trying to pull himself together. He wouldn't have thought anything of it, if it hadn't been for Moira Sanders.

Moira Sanders wasn't Hal's sort of woman. However Hal Morris was very much Moira Sanders' sort of man. And Moira Sanders had been without a man for several months now, since her boyfriend, a super-tanned car dealer called Francis had informed her that his wife was expecting him back at their villa in Cannes for the winter. Moira had subsequently discovered that the villa, and all the money Francis had appeared to have available to spend, all belonged to said wife. As a result, Moira would have to return the cashmere coat, and the Mulberry luggage and cancel the upmarket gym membership, as none of them had actually been paid for. And to pile indignity upon disappointment, her long-absent husband had also informed her that he would be seeking a divorce in order to marry his nineteen-year-old pregnant girlfriend.

So when she saw Hilly Morris, wife of the seriously dishy Hal, coming out of a seedy pub in Holborn, with a man who, although also attractive, was very definitely not her husband, she found it almost impossible to keep it to herself. Could the Morris's marriage be on the rocks? And if so, surely *she* should be the one to comfort the poor deluded Hal?

Moira felt slightly ashamed of herself for even thinking of spreading gossip. But then again, if the man was being made a fool of, he should know. It would be better to know. Livia Jenkins agreed, although to be fair, Livia Jenkins rarely disagreed with anyone or anything. But Sue Stone was another story. Sue was a campaigner, a serial signer of petitions, a constant leafleter and not averse to a spell of door-to-door canvassing on anything she felt strongly about. Most recently, she had been door-stepping houses with news of what she called intrusive garden furniture, while press-ganging shoppers into signing a petition to reduce the number of buskers in the city, and proclaiming the necessity of boot camps for obese teenagers. Sue said Moira should definitely tell Hal that his wife was cheating on him. Sue also suggested that Moira tell her when she was going to break the news. Sue felt sure she could be of help to the man, perhaps introduce him to one of her self-help groups. They were all so sadly short of men.

So when Moira ran into Hal and the twins at the Farm Shop in the village, she felt sure it was fate, not to mention Sue Stone, telling her what to do. She sidled up to him as he watched the twins patting ducks and running after chickens.

"So sweet," she said, "Little children getting to know where their food comes from. It's so important, isn't it?"

Hal watched Ben having what looked like a serious discussion with a small brown piglet. "Absolutely," he said "Although I'm not sure they've made the connection between new best friend and sausage just yet."

"You are *marvellous,*" Moira went on, "doing so much of the childcare."

"Hilly and I share the childcare."

"Do you, Do you *really?*"

"Yes," said Hal, surprised by her tone.

"I mean, as I understand it, you also have a job? A very important job?"

"I don't know about important. I do my best. Hilly's the clever one though."

"Ah yes. She used to be a lawyer, didn't she?"

"She still is a lawyer. She will be again, as soon as the girls are old enough."

"Will she? Right. I expect that would mean she was away from home quite a lot?"

"I have no idea," Hal was getting increasingly uncomfortable. What was this woman getting at?

"She stays home now though, doesn't she?" Moira continued, "Doesn't get out much. Must be hard on her."

"She's fine. We're both fine." Hal got up to go. Moira put a restraining hand on his arm.

"You wouldn't be the first," she said.

"The first what?"

"The first husband and father to find out that life with just one man, motherhood and domesticity aren't quite enough for a clever career woman."

Hal looked coldly at Moira.

"I have no idea what you mean," he said, and taking a firm hold of a twin with each hand, headed for the car, scarcely registering that one of the girls still had an equally firm grip on a large and indignant chicken. The resulting chaos in the car park exempted him from any further contact with Moira Sanders and he pretty much forgot all about it.

Until the moment he heard his wife on the phone, telling someone called Graham that he was lovely.

Chapter Twenty-Three

"What did you buy her anyway?" said Kate, as they strolled along one of the smaller canals.

"Who?"

"Laura. You said you were shopping. At the airport. When the men told you about Cassini."

"Oh. Well, it was perfume actually."

"What did you get?"

"Marc Jacobs. *Oh Lola*"

"Wow. Pricy. You people certainly like to flash the cash."

"I don't really...I mean, I hadn't done it before..it's just that I noticed she wore it before I realised.."

Kate laughed. "Don't get all fluffy on me," she said, "I only meant it was an posh gift. She'll love it. Now me, I wear something much less expensive."

She held out a wrist, and Atticus detected a faint scent of flowers and maybe something citrussy.

"Not lemon?" he said out loud.

"Almost," Kate said, "Grapefruit. They make it for me, here in Venice. In an old street just off one of the squares in Accademia. It isn't expensive, but Signora Scaachi is the only person in the world who has the recipe."

Which, Atticus realised, made it more exclusive and definitely cooler than anything he could buy from Quentin and Michael.

"So what do you think of my City?" Kate said, turning suddenly to face him and Atticus realised they were standing outside the Campanile Grande. The doorman looked slightly disapprovingly at them as they stood there, just two slightly merry, slightly dishevelled tourists, looking up at the impressive facade.

"I love it," he said to her, looking into her shining eyes, taking in the sheer enjoyment which seemed to radiate from her. "Thank you. I've had such a happy day."

"We aim to please," said Kate, stepping back and reaching into the eiderdown bag. With a flourish, she produced a stream of bubbles, which rose up into the air, and followed them by bringing out a white rabbit, which wriggled and sneezed as a bubble popped on its nose.

"How did you do that?" said Atticus amazed.

Kate put the rabbit back in the bag. "I couldn't possibly tell you."

The hotel doorman looked equally transfixed as the last of the bubbles floated away above their heads.

"I'd better go," she said, "It's almost six, and you have to get ready for your party."

Atticus's heart sank. "You're right. I'm not sure I really want to go to be honest. I wish you could come with me."

"I don't think I'd be invited," said Kate, "Don't take offence, but your Laura doesn't sound like my kind of person."

Atticus thought. She was right of course. The trouble was, he couldn't work out what that meant. Was Laura his kind of person? and if so, what had he been doing with Kate all day?

On an impulse he stepped forward and took her in his arms. He had meant to give her a hug, but somehow their lips met and he ended up kissing her rather thoroughly.

"Wow," said Kate as he drew away. "That was nice."

Atticus felt a bit dizzy. "Sorry," he said, "I shouldn't have...I didn't mean..."

"Oh, don't say you didn't mean it," said Kate cheerfully, "That would really spoil it." Seeing his downcast face, she added, "Look, we had a lovely day. You're great. Great company, You're someone else's boyfriend, someone who wears Marc Jacobs and books guests into six-star hotels just to get them to go to a party with her. I can't compete with that. But hey, you're a nice man Tix. You deserve someone special. Make sure she is, OK?"

She stepped back again, and again, until he realised she was walking away. With a little wave, she was gone.

"Pretty lady," said a voice beside him and he realised the doorman was speaking to him.

"Yes," said Atticus sadly.

"Your taxi Signore. For the Palazzo d'Artisia."

"What?"

"The taxi for the party. Is here."

"Here? *Now*?"Atticus looked at his watch desperately."Oh bugger!"

"Is alright Signore. I tell him wait. You have time."

"Good, Thank you" said Atticus, bounding into the hotel, trying frantically to find his room keycard in his inside pocket. It didn't occur to him to wonder what the doorman would think, seeing him pitch up with one girl, already late to go to a party with another one.

Apart from the time it took to find his dinner jacket in the huge room, it didn't take Atticus long to throw off the clothes he had been wearing and get himself ready to go out again. One of the great things about a) a black tie party and b) being in a hotel was that there was no choice at all over what to wear. There was also the delight of not bothering to hang anything up, worrying about whether the shirt was clean, and the limited potential for losing things, although it did take him an extra few minutes to find his cufflinks, which were zipped into the inside pocket of his holdall, a pocket which he had completely forgotten was there.

Last night's champagne was still sitting in its bucket, the label all but soaked off, and he debated whether a quick stiffener mightn't be in order before leaving, but decided that if the party went well,and Laura decided to come back for a nightcap, or if it went really badly, he could escape early and try and track Kate down. Either way, he might need it. He caught sight of himself in a long mirror debating it, a poor man's James Bond, deciding between the tall glamorous aspirational woman, and the funny clever girl. This was his kind of night. Or rather it was the man-he-had-always-wanted-to-be's kind of night.

Shutting the room door behind him again and putting the room keycard carefully into the new jacket, he was barely surprised at all when he saw Yellowhair, standing by the lift. Didn't the man possess any other clothes? Why did he still feel the need to wear them all at once?

'Evening," he said politely. Yellowhair said nothing, and as per usual, both men stared at the ceiling and then at the floor as the lift descended. Dressed like that, at least Atticus could be sure Yellowhair wasn't planing to following him to the party.

The doorman greeted him politely, as if they hadn't spoken earlier, and with a snap of his fingers, summoned a shiny wooden boat which chugged neatly round to the front of the hotel.

Atticus almost leapt down into the boat, so confident was he that he was now the man of the moment. It wasn't until they were well away from the jetty that he noticed the cello case, standing in the little cockpit with him. He looked into the cabin but there was nobody there. No cello player on the way to a recital, no final member of a quartet ready to join the other three to play at a fabulous party. No shy schoolkid dreading his first lesson, with the Italian equivalent of Miss Millard. Nobody. He hoped there hadn't been a mix-up and he hadn't been mistaken for a member of the orchestra. That he wouldn't get there, be shown to a seat on the outer edges of an orchestral semi-circle, and told to start with the Vivaldi.

He'd never actually told anyone he could play had he? He'd never said it to Laura. He hadn't even told her about the lessons. Or had he? Oh God, he *had*. Did she expect him to do a turn at this party?

The taxi chugged across the lagoon and round a corner, until St Marks Square was completely out of sight. Lowering the engine so the little boat slowed right down, the wash sank to an oily ripple behind them and there was almost no sound, as they entered a small dark channel. This Palazzo must be very exclusive, thought Atticus, it was certainly well off the beaten track. Or beaten waterway, as it were.

And then the taxi driver pulled the boat over to a low wall and killed the engine. Straining his eyes in the gloom, Atticus could just make out a little set of rather slimy looking steps. The driver nodded, indicating that he should get out.

"Look, are you sure?" Atticus said, "I mean, I don't know where I'm going. This doesn't look very likely. I'm going to the party? Party?"

"Si" said the swarthy little man, "Si. *Party*." Was it Atticus's imagination, or was there a hint of menace in his voice? He probably hated tourists. Atticus didn't want to appear touristy. He leapt out of the boat with almost as much enthusiasm as he had leapt into it, and was nearly dragged back again, as the driver fired up the engine with a roar, and swung out into the canal in a spectacular U-turn, which sent a wash up the back of Atticus's trousers.

He was completely alone. It was dark and pretty creepy. Remembering the previous parties he had been to at Laura's invitation, he tried not to be freaked out, and looked around for the nearest dark doorway, sporting a handsome if distressed handle, or subtle, expensive sign.

There was only one door, and frankly it looked more like the entrance to an east End lock-up, a warped wooden affair, with a black wrought iron handle. There were no lights, even as he stood in the street and looked up at its five or so floors.

He tried the handle. It lifted, and the door swung open. He looked round to see if there was anyone at all to ask, which was when he noticed the cello, standing on the cobbles behind him. The taxi driver must have unloaded it when he wasn't looking, presumably thinking it belonged to Atticus.

He could hardly leave it there. Someone was probably waiting for it. He picked it up, surprised by the weight of it. It seemed a long, long time since he had carried his own across town to Miss Millard's odd suburban house for his last lesson.

Once inside, the palazzo was no more inviting. Somehow this was not at all what he had expected. He was faced with a wide wooden staircase, lit by a dull single bulb overhead. Not finding any other options, he started up the stairs.

The first floor was no more helpful, nor was the second. On both, there were dark wooden doors, all locked, but the stairs went on, and so did Atticus and the cello.

As he reached the third floor, he was almost determined to give up. He would go back outside, and walk until he could find another taxi. Venice was full of these tricks, dark scary alleyways full of ghosts and shadows, just feet from lovely bright squares full of perfectly nice people and decent bars.

Then he heard music. It seemed to be coming from one of the rooms above him, so he decided to go just one more floor. Sure enough, the music got louder, some kind of light orchestral jazz, and when he tried the only door on the fourth floor, it opened, and he went in.

Atticus and the cello were standing in an empty room. It was just another room in a derelict building. He should have known by the smell, there was no party here. Nobody had lived here for many, many years. It smelled of decay, and mould, and mouse, and wet wood. In the middle of the floor, a small radio was playing the jazz. Atticus began to be very slightly frightened. He went over to the radio and picked it up. A moment later he heard the door behind him close, and then he was very, *very* frightened.

Chapter Twenty-Four

As his eyes got more accustomed to the light, Atticus could see there was a full moon outside, casting its silver beam across a small corner of the huge wooden room. He found his phone in an inside pocket and looked at its globally familiar display. Contacts, Angry Birds, Email, the BBC Weather App, they were all there. There was something incredibly reassuring about it's sameness. Except for the fact that according to the little symbols at the top, there was no signal. And almost no battery. He had completely forgotten to charge it when he checked into the hotel, and had been so excited by his day out, that it had continued to slip his mind.

He went over to the window and looked down. There wasn't much to see, but he could just make out the end of the alleyway where the boat had turned in. He could see people in brightly coloured clothes walking across the entrance to the alleyway, and almost despaired at how near they were, and yet how far away. A man, accompanied by two women in bright red evening dresses turned into the street, stopped outside the building, and pointed up at the window. Surely they could see him! Atticus banged on the glass, but it was old and thick, and too far away for the sound to reach the street. The moonlight lit up the face of the man. It was a famous face, one he had seen so many times, on the covers of magazines, on the big screen at his local Odeon. It was George Clooney. George was probably going to Laura's party. George would see him, come bounding up the stairs and let him out, and together he and Clooney would laugh about it later, at the fabulous celebrity gathering.

Then George Clooney stopped pointing and the three of them walked away. As they rounded the corner, Atticus thought he could hear laughter, but he must have imagined it.

In the quiet of Atticus's desperation, the window frame continued its centuries-old process of fading away. Flakes of soft wood came off in his hands, but as he pressed harder, he detected something more resistant underneath. Steel perhaps. The walls were soft too, and made of old fabric, which was peeling off revealing layers of straw underneath. Kate had explained that much of Venice's property was so old it was made of wood and straw, and that was why they were all so terrified of candlelight. Atticus pulled at a strip of damp silk and found that it went on and on, just tearing away with no sound.

The cello still stood by the door, like a silent guard. In what way could a cello help an innocent prisoner escape? Atticus slid to the floor and sighed. He would just have to wait until he was missed, searched for, and then rescued. He imagined Laura, in a red dress, like the one Clooney's girlfriends had been wearing, dancing with George, and probably Brad Pitt and Benedict Cumberbatch and all manner of other handsome famous men, and he could see them all in his mind, drinking champagne, and being introduced to each other, so they could think up interesting projects and do high-powered business together. All that and he wasn't there. Another life opportunity was passing him by, it was becoming a bit of a habit.

The moon crossed the sky, and the room shifted in its old creaking shell, and Atticus paced round and round, pushing at the walls, and trying the door again and again. He wondered about breaking the window, but he couldn't think how. Anyway, he was so far up, there would be no hope of escape through it. He rattled the frame in frustration. Eventually he gave up, weary of the dark and the pointlessness of his effort, and slid to the floor, his back to the door, trying to focus on the moon, while the black water flowed underneath and past and all around. The time went by and his phone beeped quietly and turned itself off, all energy spent.

Coming to with a start, he realised he had been asleep, and time had passed. The light had changed, a chilly grey dawn had filtered into the room, and looking out of the window, he could see clouds of steam rising from the canal.

He wondered what time it was, but when he went to look at his watch, it wasn't on his wrist. The absence of it was a great shock, as though he had looked down to find one of his feet was missing. He always wore his watch, it had been a gift from his Godfather Horatio, a man of immense size, immense wealth and immense generosity, chosen by Atticus's mother to represent the stability and success his father had so lacked. The watch was a large classical gold piece, which GF, as he was always known, told him was given to him by a Swiss watchmaker in a village in the mountains above Wengen in the 1940s. According to GF, it had kept near perfect time ever since, bar a single second a year, which he said was intentional, and represented the wearer's reluctance to step forward into the new year without one more, careful thought.

"Let that be your *watch-word* my boy," he had said, from what seemed to the eleven year-old Atticus a very great height, "Look before you leap. Then look once more, and then leap for all you are worth."

The loss of the watch was almost unbearable, But how could he have lost it? He had been wearing it when he came into this room, when the horrible door had closed behind him, because he remembered trying to see it in the gathering darkness. With a growing feeling of dread he checked his pockets and found that his wallet and mobile had gone too.

Staggering to his feet, stiff from the awkwardness of his dozing position, Atticus crossed the room to the door. Someone must have come in, while he was asleep and robbed him.. And it was as he got to the door, and tried the handle, that he noticed the cello wasn't there. Laughable as it most definitely was *not,* he had been burgled, while locked in an empty room.

Up until that moment, Atticus had believed he had just made a stupid mistake. He had failed to follow Laura's directions properly, hadn't checked where he was meant to be, and had taken a wrong turn somewhere. He had gone into the wrong house, and had somehow got himself locked in, probably because the door was on some sort of latch and he hadn't noticed. *Idiot*, he had thought.

But now, well how could it be some kind of random error? Because if somebody had come looking for the cello, how would they have known that he would bring it up here? And if they were just looking around in general, on the off chance that someone would carry a cello up four flights of stairs in an empty building, how could they not notice that the same someone was still in the room, trapped, not feet away from it? And if by some really bizarre chance, the cello owner had found his cello, and been so thrilled to have it back he or she hadn't asked how it had got there, or about the medium-sized chap in a dinner jacket, asleep on the floor within a cello bow's distance of it, where the hell was GF Horatio's watch?

Cursing the time he had already wasted, Atticus tried the door yet again. It was still locked. As the early morning light began to creep up the sides of the dusty old room, he noticed that the back wall of the room was not silk-lined like the others, but wood panelled. Curious, he ran his hands along the panels. Perhaps some of them would be rotten, maybe they would give way, or could be levered off with a bit of effort.

He knocked on the wooden surfaces, as he had seen people do in films, when trying to escape from victorian dining rooms, or when looking for secret rooms or hidden treasure.

Each panel sounded the same. Hollow, like a wood panel ought to really. He didn't know what he was hoping for until suddenly, about halfway along, a sharp knock resulted in a different noise, less hollow, less wooden. It was more of a dull, thick sort of thud, as though there was something pressing on the other side.

He knocked again, testing it against the one next to it. There was definitely a difference. Somehow it had to be significant. "Come on Marple," he said to himself, only fleetingly wondering why he had taken on the role of Miss Marple, rather than Poirot, or better still, Sherlock.

"Come on Marple, there has to be a way out of here," he said more loudly, to fortify himself.

He pulled and scratched at bits of wood panelling, before having a more lateral thought.

Crossing over to the window, he yanked at a piece of the frame, and got a decent sized splinter out of it. Armed with this, he went back to the panelling, and levered the splinter into a corner. With quite a bit of working, and wedging, and tugging, the panelling began to give way.

If anyone had been there to ask him, Atticus would not have been able to say what he was expecting to find behind the panelling. A hole probably. Hopefully a hole which opened out into the hallway of the building, and through which he could crawl before heading off down the stairs. Or maybe he imagined a passageway, hidden from the main building leading to the building next door, or down a chute into the street, or maybe even into a canal. Less attractive as an escape route, but an escape route nevertheless.

What he would not have said, to the imaginary person who was asking him what he was doing was, "I'm freeing this corpse from behind this panelling."

And yet that was exactly what he was doing. The panel gave way, and fell forward with a crash. For it was not a panel at all, it was the front of a crate. The whole wooden wall, which Atticus had thought was the back of the room, was in fact made up of wooden crates, stowed one on top of the other. And as this particular crate fell open, the body of a biggish man of Middle-Eastern appearance, in a purple velvet smoking jacket, tumbled into the room at Atticus's feet.

In shock he backed away, shock making him breathless. But not before he had seen who it was.

Chapter Twenty-Five

Hilly had driven too fast through London, cursing the driving rain, the grey English weather, and the traffic, as she programmed and reprogrammed the satnav to find a route to Regents' Park which wouldn't take more than seven hours. Between curses and horn sounding, and crafty moves down side streets, she could still hear Hal's words as he left the house with the twins, just that morning.

Hilly hated rowing with Hal. It didn't happen very often, and it was almost always her fault. Poor Hal, he put up with so much, and sometimes it seemed that all she did was shout at him, or nag him, or burden him with her over-active imagination. And he had been right of course, about Atticus, and that she almost certainly had no need to worry. After all, as Hal had pointed out, several times over the past two days, Atticus was a grown man, on an all-expenses paid trip to Venice with a very glamorous girlfriend, and was probably even now sipping champagne on the Rialto bridge, or sunning himself by a pool at the Lido, surrounded by awe-inspiring beauty both in terms of architecture and womanhood.

But Atticus hadn't been in touch for over twenty four hours, and his mobile just rang out, without allowing her to leave a message. Which was most unlike him. And so Hilly had been naturally a bit anxious.

"Bit anxious?" she could hear Hal protesting, "You've talked about nothing else for hours! You mollycoddle that brother of yours, no wonder he's turned off his phone. Probably to stop you ringing him every ten minutes. You've got yourself into a hell of a state for no reason!"

Which was when Hilly made her really big mistake.

"It's not for no reason!" she had shouted. "Laura Hutchinson is on the Metropolitan Police's surveillance list!"

There was a silence. Then Hal came back not the kitchen, his face pale, a long-eared woolly elephant in his hand.

"What?" he asked.

"Laura Hutchinson. That girl Atticus has gone to Venice with. She's not what he thinks. She's being watched. By the police."

"Now how on earth would you know that?" Hal said quietly.

"I...I asked Graham," Hilly confessed, realising she had gone a good deal too far.

"Graham? Graham Swann? The Graham Swann you used to hang about with when you were working? The Graham Swann you told me probably fancied you and that was why you wouldn't introduce me to him?"

"Yes" Hilly said. "He looked her up on their records."

"And why would he do that?"

"Because...because I asked him to."

"You phoned him, without telling me, and asked a man who fancies you, to help you out, without telling me?"

"I...didn't phone him. I went to see him."

Hal remembered Moira Saunders. "On the day you told me you were eating linguine with your friend Maggie?"

"Yes," said Hilly. "I would have told you, but you weren't listening to me, You said I was being paranoid, and that Atticus should just be allowed to enjoy himself. But I remembered something I'd seen in the Sunday papers, that weekend he was here, something about Laura being seen with some South African warlords, or mafia bosses or something. I put the colour supplement in the bin so he wouldn't see it in case it was just stupid tabloid gossip. But then I wished I hadn't. And I just wanted to be sure. Wanted to be reassured."

"I see," said Hal, "And so you went all the way to London, and deceived us all, and cosied up to some other man, all damsel in distress, and 'please help me my husband doesn't understand....'"

"It wasn't like that!" Hilly protested. "Anyway, I haven't deceived you *all*, as you put it. Just you. A bit. And I'm sorry."

"We're a family. What you do to one of us you do to us all," said Hal. As if on cue, Bill came trailing into the kitchen in search of the elephant. Sensing her parents' distress, she looked up at them wide-eyed. "What damsels dress?" she asked.

Hal picked her up. "I'm going out," he said.

"Don't go," Hilly protested. "We can sort this out. I just needed to know. And now I do know and I'm even more worried than before, and I know I should have told you about Graham, but I didn't and I'm sorry."

"How long have you been seeing him?"

"Hal! I am not *seeing him*. I met him just once, and then he came round, and told me about the police interest in Laura, and then I phoned him and told him there was no need to worry because Atticus was with someone else..."

"It seems you're all at it," said Hal drily, "You Drakes know how to put it about don't you?"

"Hal!" said Hilly again, "That's completely unfair!"

"I'm taking the twins to the Zoo," he said, "We'll be back by teatime. I need to be with monkeys and zebras and penguins right now."

And he had bundled Bill and Ben up in their little waterproof jackets, and strapped them into the family car, driving off without saying goodbye, which showed just how fed up he actually was. The last sight Hilly had was of one of the twins' little hands waving slightly forlornly out of the back window, and the woolly elephant, dropped in the hall, where excitement at seeing the real thing had taken over.

After standing there, shell-shocked for a moment, Hilly knew what she had to do. It was impossible to let Hal spend the afternoon thinking the worst of her, and it was entirely her fault. She would have to go after them. So she grabbed a coat, and the keys to the battered runabout which they never drove any distance, and set off in the rain to put things right.

Hal, never angry for long, had got as far as the monkey house before he started to regret taking off so hastily, not least because the twins had sensed his mood and were being somewhat less than charming. Bill had already had a mighty meltdown in the reptile house, saying she hated Izzards and Greeks and would never speak to her Daddy again unless he got her a meerkat. Meanwhile Ben had tripped and fallen into a puddle, and was now engaged in a battle of wills with her father because she wanted to take her wet dungarees off.

He knew Hilly would never cheat on him. He just knew it. He had allowed himself to be influenced by that gossipy Saunders woman who never missed an opportunity to cross the road to corner him about something or other, and had a disturbing habit of putting her hand on his arm in a proprietorial way whenever anyone else was about. And Hilly had always said that Graham Swann's feelings for her weren't reciprocated, indeed had asked Hal's advice as to how to let him down gently, because he was a friend.

The twins had spotted a camel train loping through the zoo and were demanding rides, for which they were far too young unless accompanied by an adult each, and as there was only one of him... There was no doubt about it, it was all much easier when there were two. Any minute now and there would have to be another dreaded loo visit, and he would have to face the possible dilemma over asking permission to take the girls into the Ladies' or sharing the communal changing facilities with a series of mums who invariably looked at him with either suspicion or outright lust.

It was just that Hilly and he never had secrets. They both hated them. And he couldn't understand why she had gone behind his back. But then again, he had said more than once that she was worrying unnecessarily about Atticus. What was the bloody man doing in Venice? Why couldn't he just answer his phone messages, put their minds at rest and they could all get on with the wet dreary English days, while he had a ball in the City of Dreams with goddesses. As many as he liked. Hal only wanted one goddess, and she was probably pacing the kitchen cursing him over a bottle of chardonnay by now.

The twins were now at war with each other, as one stated that Pigwigs were next on the agenda, while the other was equally determined that they should head back to see Leppids. "We have time for Pigwigs *and* Leppids" said Hal, aware of the disapproving eyes of the 'you should speak to your children as though they are adults' brigade, as he led them away, grateful that the appeal of the camel had faded.

"Mummy! Mummy!" shouted the twins, and Hal looked up to see an inquisitive boar ambling towards them through a fence. The boar regarded him with a decidedly sinister expression. "Now that's not kind," he said sternly, "It doesn't look a bit like Mummy," before he saw Hilly, wet, and flustered, wearing one of his oldest outdoor jackets, heading towards them.

"It does a bit," said Hilly, looking at the boar. "Especially its bottom. Although mine's twice the size. And I swear I found a hair growing out of my chin this morning. It's proof isn't it? I am turning into a witch."

Hal laughed, taking her in his arms. "No you're not," he said, "You are a Goddess."

"I'm sorry," they both said at once, kissing and making up with slightly more enthusiasm than the boar was used to. With a loud snort, it bashed its huge head against the fence in protest before giving up and ambling away. The twins momentarily alarmed, turned their attention to their parents. "You're *Lovering!*" shouted one, "Can we go to the Pigwigs now?"

The little family was a harmonious unit once more, and the general group hugging continued as they made their way over to the penguin pool, accompanied by the marvellous sound of sealions, barking.

"I'll go" said Hal, a couple of wet hours later, as they queued for hot chocolate and marshmallows in the Wild Safari Shack, noting that the only wild things about the Safari Shack were the length of time you had to queue for, and the prices.

"Go where?" said Hilly

"To Venice. I'll find him."

"How? How will you find him?"

"I don't know. I'll look. I'll follow any clues we have. I'll be Inspector Morse."

"Speckly Horse, Speckly Horse!" shouted the twins.

"You?"

"Why not? You can't go because the twins can't go, and besides, if Atticus is in some sort of trouble, I wouldn't want you getting mixed up in it."

"Well to be honest I wouldn't want you getting mixed up in it either!"

"I'll be fine. Although if he is just lazing about, soaking up the delights of a jet-set lifestyle, as I very much suspect, I shall find it hard to choose between hitting him and joining him"

"Well, if you really think......"

"Don't you think I can do it? Track Atticus down in a foreign city, rescue him from peril, fight off villains and bring him safely home?"

"Of course you can. Probably."

"Probably"

"Darling it's just that- lovely as you are - I've never really seen you as the heroic type."

"Well now's your chance" Hal took up a superhero pose, hooking the hood of his waterproof jacket over his head and swishing it out behind him, whilst brandishing a long-handled hot chocolate spoon.

"Silly Daddy," said Bill calmly, through a mouthful of marshmallow.

Chapter Twenty-Six

"The thing is old man," Atticus was saying, a while later, as the morning sun came up overhead. "I've no idea which way this building is facing. But given that the sun rises in the East, and that would seem to be over there, it will set in the West which, being opposite East, is going to be behind us, although of course we'll be long gone before then, At least I will be. I don't suppose you'll mind much, anyway. Bearing this in mind, I estimate it's now about eleven o clock in the morning. Presumably somebody back at the Campanile Grande, will have noticed that my breakfast hasn't been eaten. And Laura will have gone from being annoyed that I was late for her party, to livid that I didn't turn up, to pretending she doesn't care at all this morning, and now, nagging doubt will have crept in, followed by guilt that she called me all the names under the sun and perhaps I have in fact been killed or terribly injured in a freak vaporetto accident, and at about now, she will officially start to be properly worried...

"Of course she must also, I suppose, be getting a bit worried about *you*. I don't know if you made it to the party, but I'm guessing not. That jacket, although very much your usual type of thing, could scarcely be described as black tie. So where did you get to, before...well, you know, *before?"*

Boran didn't answer. His thick black hair had dust in it, Atticus noticed, as he continued to stare at the ceiling, with his beady, unseeing, black eyes.

"I hope you weren't put out by the way," Atticus continued. "I mean we weren't...Laura and I. We didn't...well we hadn't. At the time you and I met. Still haven't as it happens. Not sure what your involvement is...*was*..to be honest, but if she is... *was*...your girlfriend, of course I would never have...well you know. A decent man doesn't. Not with somebody else's girlfriend...

"So here we are. And I have to say I am sorry about you. I don't think we exactly hit it off, did we? But any friend of Laura's is a friend of mine. Ish. And anyway, I certainly wouldn't have wished this on you. But by the same token, I have to say I'm certainly not wishing it on *me*. And I am quite concerned that now that I have found you, I'm not sure where that leaves me."

Atticus stopped. His heart was beating so loudly he could hear it, but he could also hear something else. Below him, several floors below by the sound of it, he could hear movement. The floor on which he was sitting reverberated,, and as he held his breath, he could distinctly make out the low hum of people talking, and something else. The long erratic scraping sound of heavy things being dragged across a floor.

He looked up at the back of the room he was in. Here, there were crates. And downstairs crates just like these were being dragged across a floor. And the voices were those of cello burglars, watch thieves, and murderers.

Atticus sat in silence, listening to the low distant movement beneath. Of course it could all be perfectly innocent. They might be a team of builders, hired to renovate the building. He told himself that even now they were unloading ladders and erecting scaffolding poles, and pulling up floorboards to replace pipework. In a minute they would stop, having done an hour's work, and sit around with mugs of whatever Italian builders drank in place of British builders' tea, reading whatever the Italian equivalent of the *Daily Mirror* was.

And, fool that he was, Atticus was remaining trapped upstairs, when he could just as well attract their attention, get them to pop up with a crowbar and let him out, and he could give them a decent tip and a cheery wave and promise to hire them next time he was planning to redevelop a depressing Italian warehouse.

Or. They could be a team of villains, who had already done away with Boran and stuffed him into one of their crates.

Poor Laura. Whatever the nature of her relationship with Boran, she would be devastated to hear of his demise. Atticus imagined her beautiful face, a lonely tear making its way down her flawless cheek, as he held her hand and broke the news. They would be sitting on a park bench looking out across a lake as the sun went down. Or maybe they would be in his hotel room, where he could hold her close and give her champagne to make her feel better.

Laura. It was less than a month since their lunch at The Dorchester. He could remember every word she ever said to him, every look, every gesture. It was as though she had tied a fine thread round him, and was keeping him right at the end of it, pulling gently to bring him closer if he threatened to pull back. She should never have got mixed up with a man like Boran.

"There's a Party!" she had written, in her usual expansive handwriting, an invitation full of excitement and promise. *"There are people I'd like you to meet. It'll be fun!*

People she wanted him to meet. Well the only person he had actually met, was Boran, and look what had happened to *him.* Some party. Atticus wondered about the other people he had been supposed to meet. And why? Frankly why would anybody in Laura's circle of beautiful rich influential people, want to meet *him*?

He went over to the window yet again. The sun was quite bright now, and the canal flowing past the end of the street looked almost blue, compared with its usual thick brown. Painted gondolas bobbed past, and streams of tourists with backpacks took pictures of themselves and each other with their phones. Sometimes it seemed as though they were looking right up at him, as they marvelled at the seedy old buildings in this part of the City. But what part of the City *was* this?

Kate would know. Atticus felt a pang of sadness. Kate would have got him out of this. She would have done a magic escaping trick and they would have been out on the cobbles and off to a jolly good lunch before another moment had passed, complete with a performing seal if that had been the mood she was in.

He wondered if Kate would be looking for him. Maybe she had turned up at the hotel hoping to hear all the gossip about George Clooney and Brad Pitt and Benedict Cumberbatch. She wouldn't take no for an answer. If she didn't find him, she would search. That was the kind of girl Kate was.

He remembered kissing her outside the hotel. That was quite a kiss. He remembered her scent, that flowery grapefruit thing that they only made in some side street. Then he looked at Boran. Atticus had never imagined how absolutely still a dead person would be. There was, he realised, the possibility that he would never kiss Kate again. Or Laura for that matter, or anyone else. He would never see Hilly and Hal and the twins, and they would grow up remembering him as some shadowy figure who arrived with mad exploding presents and bottles of mummy and daddy's special juice. Atticus felt a lump in his throat at the thought of two little girls in dungarees asking where Uncle Hatticus was.

If he didn't get out of here alive, he would never be able to find Flora, and make it up to her. Until now, he hadn't been able to imagine how such a thing would be possible, couldn't think of anything he could ever say which would make it alright. Now, sitting in this remote corner of a strange city, trapped with a dead body and a team of evil builders, he began to realise that saying almost anything to Flora might just be better than saying nothing.

He pulled another strip of silk off the wall, and wrapping it round a finger, wrote in the dust on the floor beside him, a list of things he would do if he made it through this.

Say Sorry to F

Hug Twins

Tell Hilly who really set fire to her wendy house

Have another proper go at learning to play the cello

Kiss Laura again

Kiss Kate again

Marry one of them

He was seriously hungry. Maybe he would die of starvation before he was murdered. Would that be better?

There was no sound from the floors below, and the only movement he saw in the street was a scruffy dog, nosing about in doorways, looking for interesting things to smell. At one point the dog looked up, and Atticus looked back. "Get me some help," he said to the dog, "Be the sort of dog that rescues people."

But the dog turned and scampered away. Atticus tried to pretend he wasn't in danger of sending his days in a locked room with a corpse. How long did it take before a dead body began to smell? Or until it started to attract things which would eat it? He was thirsty too, and tired, and frightened. Would there come a point when he was so hungry, *he* would start to think about eating Boran? Depressed and dejected, he sat by the window again, telling himself he would get his breath back, and try again to escape.

It must have been an hour or so before he woke again, surprised that he could sleep at all in the circumstances. He felt oddly sick, as though he had a hangover, which was scarcely possible, given that it was twenty four hours since yesterday lunchtime. He was no longer twenty he reflected ruefully, sleeping rough was not something he had ever planned on doing again, after his last Festival, when he had woken up with his head in a puddle at Glastonbury fifteen years ago.

He rubbed his right arm which was stiffer and more sore than the rest of him. As his head cleared he remembered Boran, and turned to see that the room was empty. Boran, and the wall of crates from which he had fallen, were gone.

Surely it wasn't possible that anyone could sleep through the removal of a dozen or so wooden crates and a dead body, and not wake up at all? And if someone - people - had come and moved Boran, why didn't they find Atticus?

Then another thought occurred to him. If they - whoever they were - knew he was there, they would know he had found Boran. And if they knew *that*...

There was nothing for it. He would have to get out. And get out now. Brushing himself off. he went over to the door. He tapped on all its panels, and found the heavy wood to be as solid as ever. He crouched down and peered through the keyhole. It was blocked from the other side, presumably with the key.

Atticus had seen films in which prisoners slid paper under a locked door, pushed the key through, and pulled paper and key back underneath. But the only paper he could find was an old coffee shop receipt in the pocket of his dinner jacket. It was dated three years ago, presumably the last time he had worn the jacket. The receipt was approximately three inches square and offered him a free coffee next time he visited.

It might work. He smoothed the receipt out, and started to feed it under the door, roughly under the keyhole. The he heard footsteps in the hall outside. He froze. The paper had gone all the way through, there was no way he could retract it. Of course. He should have written on it. He should have written a message, *Help Me*, or *I'm Trapped*. How *stupid*.

Atticus rummaged in his jacket again, hoping for another chance, but he knew there would be no more receipts. And then the footsteps stopped. There was a slight pause, and then the door handle turned. Atticus ran across the room and backed against the window. If all else failed, he would jump.

"*Darling!*"said a musical voice. "Whatever are you doing in here?"

Chapter Twenty-Seven

Laura was standing in the doorway, her long legs in high heeled boots, casting a statuesque shadow against the wall behind her. Her amazing white-gold hair cascaded over the shoulders of a beautiful coffee-coloured suede coat. She looked incredible, and to Atticus's tired and hungry brain, like an angel.

"I - er I got shut in. By accident," he said. "I was on the way to your party. As you see." He indicated the dinner jacket, now crumpled and dusty beyond recognition. "I'm sorry I didn't make it. It's been a bit of an ordeal actually. Bloody stupid to leave these old empty buildings unlicked and then let people get shut in. And I can tell you this is not a good place to be hanging around in. I'm surprised you're even here."

"Why didn't you just leave?" said Laura laughing at him.

"It was locked," he said, indicating the door.

"Of course it wasn't," said Laura, "see?" And she showed him the door on both sides. There was no locking mechanism. The lock had been taken cleanly out.

"Probably one of those beautiful old venetian locks," she said, "They're in great demand, thieves sell them in the markets. I expect some vandal went through the whole building, removing them. He'll make a tidy profit, when someone eventually decides to renovate this horrible old building and has to buy them all back."

"They *are* renovating this building actually," said Atticus, trying to make sense of what she was saying. "I heard the works going on downstairs. But given the kind of area this is, who knows what they were up to."

"You're right," said Laura, "this is a very undesirable bit of town. There's no sign of any building work."

"I was afraid of that." said Atticus, realising he wasn't surprised.

"Anyway Babe, why are you still standing there? Why don't we just get out of here, and I'll buy you a very late lunch to make up for what you've been through. You know, you seem really upset."

Atticus *was* really upset. Something was still bothering him. He shook his head which still felt as if it was full of cotton wool. He felt as though he had been taking sleeping pills. But of course he hadn't. He was annoyed that Laura didn't seem to be taking him seriously. "How did you know I was here?" he asked after a pause.

""I missed you at the party! I was terribly tied up, you know how it is, all these people needing me, but when I couldn't find you at all, I asked if anyone had seen you, and someone suggested you might have gone and got yourself lost, and eventually Gorgeous George said he thought he just might have seen you, all the way out here."

"So it *was* him, thought Atticus. She really did know everybody.

"He's looking for some development projects, planning to start up a film studios, terribly exciting" Laura was continuing, "Anyway, *I* said don't be ridiculous, what would Atticus be doing in an empty building in such a *beastly* bit of town, and he said perhaps you were looking to buy a building too. *Are* you Darling? It would be terribly exciting. I could put you in touch with some very interested people."

"I don't think...." began Atticus, "It isn't really me....."

"*Later* Darling" Laura broke in. "Now we need that lunch!"

"Lunch?" repeated Atticus.

"Yes. We still have time. You missed the party, you deserve a Bellini at least. As do I. I have a killer hangover" She held out a hand, glittering with diamond rings. "Such a shame you missed the party. It was a *blast!*"

Atticus headed for the open door tentatively, half expecting to find it had all been a mirage, and he would find it locked as before, that he had imagined Laura and the sunlight, and the possibility that he could get out. Then, as he crossed the room he remembered Boran. Oh God, he was going to have to break the news to Laura. She would be devastated.

"The thing is," he began, "Dear thing, I have to tell you something. Something you will probably find rather sad."

Laura laughed. "*Later*" she said again, "Later. We have to get you a drink. Although if we're going to Ziferelli's, we're going to need to go via what passes in this mad City for Savile Row."

"Rue D-Ivola?" said Atticus, surprised at the memory's ability to conjure up small detail in a crisis.

"That's it," said Laura, surprised. "It's the only place, and I'm going to treat you to a jacket. Even Ziferelli might raise an eyebrow at the state of that one."

Laura, smiling, radiantly beautiful, rich, welcoming, *fun*. How wrong could it be? Atticus's righteous indignation abated a little and he headed towards the door, still very slightly expecting it to close in front of him.

Half an hour later, Atticus stood in front of a long mirror in a crisp new white T-shirt and a powder-blue cashmere blazer. He had never worn a jacket over a T-shirt before, he felt somehow underdressed, as if he'd forgotten a layer.

"You know I never would have imagined, all those years go at St Joe's, that you would turn out to be quite so gorgeous," Laura said, her head on one side, looking at her own reflection in the mirror.

Atticus, embarrassed, tried not to look at the male shop assistant, who was obviously trying to suppress his credulity, as he packed Atticus's filthy dinner jacket into one of the shop's trademark burgundy boxes.

"I think we need a sweater too," Laura said, moving round the shop and browsing through a selection of fine merino knitwear in all the colours of boiled sweets.

"I think I'll be quite warm enough in this jacket," said Atticus, wondering what Hilly would say if she saw him in this colour.

"No silly, it's not to *wear*," said Laura, "It's to *drape*. She picked a salmon pink sweater from the pile and wrapped it round Atticus's shoulders. There she said, you look quite Italian!"

Atticus thought he looked quite ridiculous, but he was in no position to argue. Laura had already handed over her credit card, and was halfway out of the shop before she turned back.

"Loafers," she said, "You must have loafers."

"Cassini," said the assistant. "Is two doors on from here."

"Please," said Atticus, in desperation, "You've done so much already. Why don't we just go straight to lunch? The thing is, I do rather need to talk about what's been happening to me, and there's something I really have to tell you."

Laura hesitated. "No" she said, "I really can't have you running about Venice in those old man's shoes" She looked at Atticus's black dress shoes, which he had to agree had seen better days, and which had not come through their warehouse ordeal terribly well. "Come on," she said, and before he knew it, he was inside the shop where Jerome was just finishing wrapping a pair of pale pink moccasins for a swarthy man in an anorak.

Praying that Jerome hadn't had a good enough look at him through the window two days ago, while Kate had been being so forceful about his music lessons, Atticus kept his head down, while Laura chose between pale grey and dark green loafers. Just as she had made up her mind to go for the green, a third pair, in a sort of two-tone cream and gold caught her eye, and Atticus looking out of the window miserably, saw Yellowhair, standing in a doorway on the other side of the road, staring in at him.

"I say," Atticus said to Laura, "Do you know that man?"

"What man Babe?" said Laura, indicating that Jerome should box up Atticus's dress shoes "There's nobody there."

And by the time Atticus looked back, there wasn't anyone in the doorway.

"It's just that, I know it seems odd, but I think I'm being followed," he said, as Laura took his arm.

"I've told them to send your old things back to the hotel," she said, leading Atticus out of the shop, Now don't be an old fusspot.Venice *is* a bit creepy isn't it? That's why I love it. All ghosts and strange happenings. Look at you, staying in a horrid old warehouse for a whole 24 hours, and not realising the door wasn't even locked! You'll be telling me you've seen a dead body in the canal next!" She led him up a side street to a very elegant little bar.

Dead body, thought Atticus, seeing Boran's staring eyes looking up at the ceiling.

"This is Ziferelli's" Laura said, "I love it. It's ludicrously pricy of course, but then all the best things are aren't they?"

Atticus thought with a pang about Kate, and the little pizzeria.

Chapter Twenty-Eight

Laura was welcomed in the usual effusive way by the staff, headed by the surprisingly short and round Ziferelli himself, a balding man with a moustache which could well have been fake. As they kissed and fawned over one another, Atticus surveyed the room. He realised one could quickly tire of urban chic.

Ziferelli's was a long, narrow room, furnished almost completely in glass. The bar, which was L-shaped in the middle of the room was glass, so that the wine glasses and bottles appeared to be suspended in mid air, while the transparent tables disappeared between the diners, leaving their plates and drinks similarly floating. It was very unnerving. Atticus rather longed for tablecloths, and candles in bottles. Or a retro leather armchair, and a pile of weeks-old Sunday supplements inviting a good read over a glass of Bordeaux.

Laura seemed deep in conversation with yet another impossibly handsome man at another table and Atticus began to wonder if he could decently leave. Despite the new clothes, he felt grubby, as if he hadn't had a bath for a very long time, which of course he had not. He was tired and anxious. He was also sure he had seen Yellowhair in that doorway, and if he had, the man was definitely following him. There was no way that so many sightings, even in such a small, densely packed city as this, could be coincidence. After all, he hadn't seen Kate for ages, and he really wished *she* was following him.

A waiter brought a long glass filled with a pinkish liquid and set it on the table in front of him. "Is Bellini" he said, pointing at it. "Better than Cipriani."

Atticus looked at the drink. It looked rather like bathwater. He raised it to his lips to discover that it smelt rather more like washing-up water. It was scented, but not entirely floral, rather more like over-ripe fruit, left too long in the fruit bowl. He felt a bit sick, and suddenly realised that as well as hunger and tiredness, he was also, somewhere deep inside, just a little bit fed up.

"Atticus doesn't get angry," Hilly was fond of saying. "That's his fundamental problem. He's too nice. He just gets a little miffed." Oh, for Hilly, thought Atticus, with her quick temper and equally quick recovery, famous for her ability to shout a stream of unladylike abuse at a lorry driver who carved her up on a motorway, and then in the same breath, continue with the third verse of *All Things Bright and Beautiful,* which for some inexplicable reason, the twins loved. Hilly had always been able to release her feelings, and Atticus had always been envious of it.

But now, as he sat there, dressed in pale blue and draped with a salmon pink sweater, his two-tone shoes squeaking loudly as he flexed his toes, apparently being ignored by Laura, he realised that was he was really missing, was *himself.* No Godfather Horatio's watch, no phone, with its little store of past messages from home, and no idea what was going to happen next. If there was an Atticus he wanted to be, he wasn't being it.

Laura was indicating across the room, and as he looked at her, she mouthed words which looked like

'Back in a few minutes' and blew him a kiss, before disappearing through a door at the back of the bar, followed by the handsome Italian.

Atticus stood up. He realised he was shaking, but whether it was due to the hunger, or his recent adventures, he had no idea. He was going to leave. He really was. As he stood up, he looked out of the window, and to his amazement there was Kate. At least he was pretty sure it was Kate. She was wearing the Harlequin mask they had bought in Accademia just 48 hours or so ago. It seemed like a lifetime. But, yes, it was definitely Kate. She was waving at him, and he crossed the room to the door at lightning speed, almost knocking over an invisible table.

"It *is* you!" he said, in amazement, as they met on the steps.

Kate rummaged in the eiderdown bag and produced a small bunch of plastic daffodils which she gave to the waiter who had followed Atticus, believing him to be escaping without paying his bill. The waiter, confused, faded away.

"Of course it's me. Good God what *are* you wearing?" Kate said, laughing. "You look like, well let me think what *do* you look like. A kingfisher. Or a birthday cake. Or..."

"An idiot," finished Atticus. "I know. My clothes got, well, Laura,...."

"Ah," said Kate, wisely. "*Her* choice. She really is something, isn't she? Those *shoes*! Cassini, I presume?"

"Cassini," said Atticus.

"I'll have to speak to Jerome. He should never have let *that* happen. The boy has no sense of responsibility. Anyway, come along, we have lots to catch up on. I want to hear all about the party! I'm assuming, that because you are now dressed entirely in Laura's idea of 'man' clothes, you haven't been back to your hotel room to collect yours? Bad boy!"

"It's not what you think," said Atticus. "In fact it is so far from what you think that I suspect you just won't believe me when I tell you."

"You know you'd be surprised what I believe," said Kate, "I'm well aware of the magic that can occur in a place like this, both good and bad."

"Look," said Atticus, looking round furtively and taking Kate's arm, expecting Laura to appear at any moment. "Is there somewhere we can go? Somewhere where we can talk?"

"What about Laura?"

"Oh, she won't notice. I suspect she's busy with some of her strange friends. I can leave her a note. If I can find something to write on. And a pen."

He patted the pockets of his new jacket optimistically, realising he had nothing.

Kate, elbow deep in the eiderdown bag, produced both a pen and paper in an instant, but not before Atticus had been able to see quite a way into the bag. Right down at the bottom there was a seething mass of gold chains, sparkling jewellery, mobile phones and leather purses.

"Good God," he said, "That bag's full of...."

"Treasure," said Kate firmly. "All well deserved. Now get on with that note."

"I wish I could 'find' treasure," Atticus said, realising he was in essence encouraging petty crime. "Instead, I seem to have become very good at losing things. I don't suppose you've come across my Godfather Horatio's watch on your travels?"

He turned to find a flat surface on which to write his note to Laura, but as he did so, Kate produced something from the bag. "Is this it?" she said, holding it up.

There was a long silence.

"How could you....?" said Atticus.

"I wondered if it was yours when I saw it," said Kate, calmly. "I always notice people's things. You know, jewellery, watches etc. I never take things people care about, just Rolexes and pretty trinkety things and stuff people are careless with. This is quite out of my usual remit. But when I saw it, it reminded me of you. So I took it."

"But where was it? When you took it?"

"Some guy was wearing it. Some guy who had clearly nicked it from *you*.This town really needs cleaning up, the crime rates are inexcusable."

Atticus put the watch back on, lovingly feeling his way along the holes in the worn strap, stroking the face of it, vowing to be a great deal more careful of it in future.

"I can't believe you found - stole - it," he said. "I thought I'd never see it again. What did he look like, this guy?" he asked.

"Oh I can't remember," said Kate. "Biggish, dark, a bit swarthy to be honest. It didn't suit him at all. He's much more the gold Rolex type. Or those huge adventure watches, you know, the ones that cost thousands and you can go diving in them only nobody ever does, and if you did, they're so heavy you'd probably never get back up to the surface again."

"Yes, never mind the watch," said Atticus, almost impatiently, "the man?"

"Oh yes. *Him,*" said Kate, who seemed to have lost interest. "Does it really matter? I got it back for you. Now that certainly deserves a drink. I didn't even get to go to your stupid party and all the time I was looking after you anyway, which is more than can be said for Leggy *Oh Lola* Laura"

"You're right," said Atticus. "I do owe you a drink, only...."

"Let me guess," said Kate, "You haven't got any money. Wallet too eh? I should have done old Omar over a bit more thoroughly, shouldn't I? Never mind, I'll treat us. Or someone will. I haven't decided who yet."

"Wait!" said Atticus, "Omar. You said Omar."

"Yes. Sharif. That's who he reminded me of. You know, the git who stole your watch. Hope the police catch up with him and he gets what he deserves."

"Oh I'm sure of it," said Atticus, wondering if he should add a gentle postscript to his note for Laura, about finding Boran murdered in a crate in a disused warehouse. Probably not, he decided and instead he wrote:

Sorry Darling, you've been so kind, but I'm a bit bushed. Back to hotel for a wash and brush up, and perhaps we can meet later? You know where I am. PS. Thank you for jacket etc. xx"

"Nice." said Kate, looking over his shoulder. "I think the pink glitter felt pen and *Country Diary of an Edwardian Lady* notepaper set exactly the right tone, don't you?" And she replaced the rest of the notepad and the pen in her bag. "Now," she said, "where shall I take you for proper drinks?"

"Somewhere quiet and inconspicuous," said Atticus, "I know it sounds daft, but I have this distinct feeling I'm being followed."

"Well if you are, you've just made it a whole lot easier," said Kate, looking him up and down.

"You're not leaving are you?" cried Laura, suddenly appearing behind Atticus and Kate with rather more swooping than was entirely comfortable, "I know I've neglected you badly, I'm *dreadful* aren't I?" She looked rather pointedly at Kate with a look which seemed to indicate that it was Kate who was dreadful. "Aren't you going to introduce me to your friend?"

Atticus felt distinctly hot under the salmon pink merino collar. "Absolutely," he said, trying to sound firm. "Kate, this is Laura Hutchinson, my...."

"Girlfriend!" finished Laura smoothly. Atticus looked at her in amazement. "I don't think we've quite got to that stage..." he began but nobody was listening. Kate had disappeared.

"Kate?" said Atticus desperately, Kate?"

"Oh dear," said Laura sounding distinctly pleased with herself, "I'm afraid she's gone. What a pity. Now let's go in and enjoy our lunch. Ziferelli has rustled up the perfect *Coniglio Con Lattuga*."

Atticus was torn. He really wanted to go after Kate, but Laura had a decidedly firm grip on his arm. Before he knew it he had turned to go back into the restaurant. Laura's lovely face had softened again, and he found himself weakening under her ice-blue gaze.

"Don't disappoint me Babes," she said, pouting, "I *need* you!"

I doubt that, thought Atticus. Then he heard a whisper, behind his right ear.

"Don't turn round," whispered Kate. "Come away with me!"

"What exactly is *Coniglio Con Lattuga*?" he asked out loud, to cover his confusion.

Laura laughed. "Rabbit," she said. "In liquorice."

If there was anything Atticus liked less than the idea of eating rabbits, it was the taste of liquorice. "Oh great," he said, "My favourite."

"Liar," whispered Kate. "Poor little bunnies!"

"I have champagne waiting," purred Laura.

"*I* have the best spaghetti and a bottle of red," whispered Kate. "No woodland creatures were harmed in the making of lunch at Pete's."

"There are some people I really want you to meet," Laura continued.

"Just you, and me and Pete's Pasta?" hissed Kate. She was very close, but he just couldn't see her.

"We can ask George about the film studio. He'll *love* you," said Laura.

"George?" said Atticus out loud.

"Clooney," said Laura. "He's over there, at his usual table."

"Oh. My. God, *Go*!" whispered Kate "You must *Go*! You'll get to meet George *Clooney*! I'll catch you later!"

"Wait!" said Atticus, turning to where Kate's voice had come from.

"What?" said Laura, still doing dinky little finger waves across the room, to where a trio of dark-suited men was sitting. "Who are you talking to?"

"I was just...It was....." Atticus began, going back to the doorway.

"Don't be tiresome Atticus," said Laura in a suddenly chilling voice. He was suddenly reminded of the Ice Queen in Narnia. He realised he had almost fallen for the Turkish Delight which CS Lewis's wicked Queen had offered Edmund, and which had been his downfall. "I'm sorry," he said to Laura, "I really do have to go."

"No!" said Laura in a voice like a pistol shot.

But what Atticus heard *was* a pistol shot.

Chapter Twenty-Nine

There was an incredible silence. An awe-inspiring, shattering silence, which lasted hours, maybe years. Nobody moved. When he came round, Atticus realised he had somehow been thrown against the door frame, and had landed awkwardly on the steps into the restaurant. Struggling to his feet, the first thing he noticed was that the merino sweater had snagged on a rusty doornail.

The second thing he noticed was that Laura was lying on the floor, beside him, one foot twisted underneath her, both arms outspread. Her air was flowing down the steps like a river of gold, washing the life of Laura Hutchinson away and down the street, while her pale eyes, almost colourless now, stared upwards. A deep, dreadful red stain was spreading across the front of her cream silk blouse, radiating outwards from where her heart had been beating, just seconds earlier.

And still there was silence. Atticus waited, unable to move. As if in slow motion, people began to gather round, leaving their tables and moving closer, while waiters ran from all corners towards the doorway. Ziffirelli made his way through the incredulous crowd, stepped daintily over the body and quietly closed the door to the street, clipping the ends of Laura's hair as he did so, pushing her head aside slightly to get the bolt across. Another waiter brought a large white tablecloth, and laid it over Laura. No longer able to see those dreadful sightless eyes, Atticus finally looked up to find that everybody seemed to be looking back at him.

"I didn't..." he began, "It wasn't.....I have no idea... who *did* this? Who would *do* this? My God, you *can't* think.....?!"

Ziferelli took his arm. "Come with me," he said, in a chilling voice not unlike that of Marlon Brando in the Godfather.

"I don't want to go with you!" said Atticus, "The police! We need to call the police. Has someone called the police?" His voice rose in panic, "I don't *want* to go with you!" he protested once more, as he was steered very firmly away from the door, through the restaurant and towards the back of the room. He was vaguely aware that the table at which George Clooney and his friends had apparently been sitting was now empty. Presumably film stars were kept out of the way of unpleasantness, such as diners being murdered on the doorstep.

Atticus was propelled roughly through the door, and he found himself in the kitchen of Ziferelli's restaurant. At least he assumed it was the kitchen. There was a great expanse of stainless steel and a very high number of sinks, but a surprising lack of activity, for what had until moments before, been a very busy lunch service. Half a dozen youths in chef's whites stood around idly, whilst another was ripping open packets which appeared to have been delivered from a well-known supermarket.

"This way," said Ziferelli, not letting up as he applied pressure to Atticus's arm.

"But I didn't...! I"m *not*...I was just standing there, She was my *friend*!" he protested.

Ziferelli stopped.

"Well, not exactly, friend," said Atticus desperately, "just someone, I mean I've known her for years, well not exactly for years, just years ago. And then again recently, I mean we barely saw each other, I would never, and anyway, I'm *British!* We don't go round shooting each other. Well not many of us do......"

Ziferelli continued with their journey, until they got to another door. This one was huge, and made of steel, and with a vast iron bolt across it. With surprising strength for one so short, he hauled the bolt across and opened the door. It was decidedly dark on the other side. "Look here!" shouted Atticus, "You can't do this to me! I have rights! I'm a European citizen! I need representation. Where is the ambassador?"

With a firm shove in the small of his back, Ziferelli propelled Atticus through the door,and slammed it shut. Atticus heard the bolt being pushed back across on the other side, and then there was silence, except for the massive thundering noise made by the beating of his heart.

Before his eyes accustomed themselves to the dark, the first thing Atticus was aware of was a deep, chilling cold. The second thing he noticed was the smell. It was powerful, pungent,, sort of organic, not entirely unpleasant, and vaguely familiar. He tried to establish what it was, putting his hands out in front of him and then to either side. Both hands made contact, his right finding hard wood, his left landing on an altogether softer surface, something spongy, slightly sticky. The smell got a good deal stronger. Clearly this was a very small room, and he was not on his own in it.

His eyes began to get more used to the lack of light, and he could gradually make out shelving on either side of where he stood, with a variety of oddly shaped objects, stacked, floor to ceiling. He wiggled the fingers of his left hand, and some more sticky softness came away. Dreading what he would find he looked down at his hand.

It was cheese.

Atticus was in   Ziferelli's cheese larder. He almost laughed, until he realised the predicament he was in. The temperature couldn't be more than 8 degrees, and the air was damp. He was, in effect, sitting in a fridge. At first, he thought the only light was coming from a crack under the heavy door he had come through, but as he scanned the tiny space, he realised that there was another line of light, at floor level, in front of him. With a burst of something approaching joy, he realised it must be another door.

He stepped forward and put out a hand. It met a cold, flat surface, but as he ran it up and down, he felt a simple metal handle of the kind you could pick up in a DIY shop. He pressed on it, and it gave. There was a click, and miraculously, the door swung open.

Now Atticus found that he was actually laughing. It was all just so ridiculous. The pale blue jacket was covered in what looked like dust, but could well be powdered cheese rind, the salmon pink sweater was pulled so out of shape it resembled a dishcloth, and he smelt strongly of dolcelatte. Two people he knew had been murdered, one left in a locked room with him, the other gunned down while she was standing next to him. However bad he looked and smelled, *it* looked and smelled worse.

But on the other hand, he was standing in an alleyway at the back of the restaurant. There was nobody in sight, and nobody to stop him just walking away. All he had to do was decide which way to go.

"Signor!" a voice said, striking a chill into his bones. "Signor! You must not go without your instrument!"

He turned to see one of the waiters from Ziferelli, coming towards him down the alleyway. The man was carrying the a cello case. "Ees valuable" the man said, handing it over. "Ees belong to Lady."

"The lady? The one who was..well, who was..."

"Non! said the man, "Not the shiny lady who is dead. The other lady. The magic lady."

Kate, thought Atticus. The cello must be Kate's. Which was odd, because she had never mentioned it. Then again he could quite believe she was a brilliant musician as well as everything else. Music and magic, they seemed to go together in this extraordinary City. Perhaps that was why she had come to live here. He had never asked her.

Feeling terribly guilty about Laura, whilst at the same time trying to erase the memory of her cold, lifeless body on the steps of Ziferelli's, Atticus picked up the cello.

"You must run away," said the waiter suddenly. "They come for you. Because of dead lady. They come for you!"

Atticus looked up. Blue lights lit up the deck of a small white police launch which was approaching, sweeping up the canal which ran along the end of the street, sending a bow wave spilling over into the street, heading towards him. Atticus turned and ran.

Or rather he trotted. It was, Atticus discovered, very difficult to run while carrying a cello. He had forgotten how heavy cellos were. He was sure his own instrument didn't weigh anything like as much. but then again it had been a long while since he last carried his cello any distance, and anyway, perhaps Kate's was a superior cello. Perhaps even a famous one, a Stradivarius, or an Amati. The new loafers squeaked, as he made his way up one side street and down another, always choosing the route least likely to attract attention, slipping in and out of dark shadows, and hoping that if he just kept going he would eventually find himself somewhere he recognised. His feet twisted on the cobbles, and the shoes began to pinch. You didn't need leather shoes for a job like this he thought, you needed trainers. Those huge bouncy white things so beloved of American tourists, who even now were pottering around St Mark's Square buying souvenirs and eating triple-decker burgers and gigantic pizzas, taking pictures of pigeons, and just enjoying their lives, oblivious to the trouble he was in.

He paused for a minute at the corner of a tiny square, to catch his breath. There was nobody in the square except for a pair of incredibly old men playing backgammon at a tin table, and an equally prehistoric crone in a black cloak, sitting on the steps of the inevitable church, a basket at her feet.

Atticus contemplated going into the church Perhaps there he might find some sanctuary, maybe even some help. Should he confess? He felt guilty but it was difficult to know what he was actually guilty of. Perhaps God would sort all that out. Or perhaps a kindly clergyman would be able to advise him as to what he should do.

As if sent from heaven, a priest in long robes came out of the church at that very moment. He looked both ways and crossed himself, as another man in a very loud pinstriped suit came over to him. The two exchanged words, and an envelope which looked suspiciously like the sort which contained bundles of unmarked cash, changed hands. The pinstriped man walked away, and the priest extracted something from the envelope and put it in the crone's basket. Then, checking that nobody had seen him, he went back inside the church. The crone stood up, picked up her basket and with a surprisingly rapid step, left the square. Atticus decided against asking the Lord for help. Was everybody up to shady deeds in this city?

How had he got into this mess? He had been in Venice just a few days, but time had seemed suspended, to the point where he could barely remember his life before coming here. He thought back to Laura and the lunch at the Dorchester. How happy he had been to be distracted from his dull, going-nowhere life, by her exciting invitations and strange mysterious friends. Then there had been that party in Mayfair. He had even gone back a few days later, curious and suspecting he had dreamt the whole thing, and was told the building was near derelict, and being squatted in by a bunch of art students. As if to prove a point, a bunch of young people in paint-spattered clothes and heavy boots appeared, carrying a huge and very graphic painting between them.

He should never have accepted Laura's invitation to come to Venice, he saw that now. How suspicious it was, a beautiful, sexy, successful woman offering him an all-expenses trip just for the pleasure of his company. No, there had to be more to it than that. And he, through a combination of boredom, vanity and naivety had fallen for it. Now he saw that Laura had clearly got herself mixed up with a very bad crowd, possibly someone she was working for, providing her 'important introductions' and presumably she had been taken in, just as he had been. Poor Laura. And if she had hoped he would rescue her, well he had completely and utterly failed her. He couldn't even find his way to a party without getting himself locked in a warehouse with a dead body. And now poor Laura was dead too. But who was behind it all? And what was '*it*'?

A small group of schoolgirls in very short uniform skirts passed him, giggling and attending to their phones with rapt attention. Atticus tried to hide behind the cello case, but in any case they didn't look up, although one of them muttered 'giacca bello' under her breath as they passed, and they all burst into hysterical giggles. Their young bright voices rang out as though murder and death didn't even exist, just a few streets away.

It was almost five in the afternoon. The sun had already gone from many of the smaller Venetian squares, and the streets were shadowed, providing useful cover for Atticus, who was seriously tiring of lugging the cello around trying to find his way back to the Campanile Grande, without being seen by any passing policemen or murderers. He began to feel a bit uncharitable. Really, Kate might have taken her own bloody cello. Dreams of a wonderful future in which they travelled the world playing soulful classical duets in the great concert halls were fading in favour of dreams of a hot bath and a pair of shoes which didn't feel as though they were sawing his toes off.

The inevitable groups of loitering tourists were both a help and a hindrance to Atticus, as he wound his way around them. For every useful group of well-fed Americans in bulky outerwear looking upwards and providing useful cover, there was a stream of thin, sickly- looking Chinese children, intent on taking as many photographs of themselves as they could and providing a very real challenge as to how he could pass without appearing in any of the shots. He trailed over a small bridge, the soles of the new shoes now really burning his feet. He was beginning to despair. Would he ever get back to the hotel, and if he did, would the police be waiting for him? Or worse, would Laura's killer be here, ready to cut him down where he stood, baby-blue jacket, and cello notwithstanding?

"Pssssst! Signore!" He heard a voice which seemed to be coming from under his feet. He stepped aside.

"Am down 'ere. Crosso the breedge."

Atticus did as he was told, and turned to look underneath, where a very small and tatty gondola was bobbing up and down, seemingly unmanned.

"Hello?" he said.

"Signore! I will 'elp. Get in the boat," said the voice.

Now at this point, Atticus knew he should do anything, anything at all, except get in the boat. The last time he had got into a boat he had ended up locked in a disused warehouse with a corpse. And he was beginning to think that the mistake might not have been entirely of his own making. Inadequate directions, maybe. A wrong turning up a side street, maybe, even the simple misunderstanding about the kind of disused warehouse in which you have a really cool party and the kind of warehouse in which you leave crates full of murder victims. But all of them at once? And now Laura had got caught up in it all, and she was dead. And a boat was talking to him.

But his feet really hurt. And the cello was very heavy. And as he looked back the way he had come, he realised two things; that he had already crossed this very bridge at least once in the other direction, and that two men in police uniform were heading his way. What was it Kate had said, you can rely on gondoliers, to get you out of trouble?

Atticus got in the boat. Immediately, a stringy youth in the gondoliers' uniform of striped T-shirt, beribboned hat and black trousers jumped in beside him and unhooked the rope which was holding the boat to the bridge.

"You go under the shit" he said to Atticus. Initially alarmed, Atticus realised he meant the tarpaulin which was covering the boat's central seat. He bent down and looked under it, gingerly. He could see nothing, but there was a distinct smell of fish. He hesitated, uncertain, but then he noticed the two uniformed officers peering over the bridge above him and dived under the smelly canvas, dragging the cello with him. Lying there in the dark, he could see nothing, but he could feel the rocking of the boat, and hear the lapping of the water on the wood, just inches from his ears. He thought he felt something slimy brush his cheek.

After a few minutes, he plucked up enough courage to lift a corner of the tarpaulin and peep out. From his position flat in the bottom of the gondola he could see the feet of the gondolier, grubby white plimsolls, some distance from the flapping wide-legged trouser hems, revealing a good four inches of pale leg, bluish skin peppered with swarthy black hair. That was odd he thought, having hitherto believed that gondoliers were a reasonably proud lot, keeping both themselves and their boats in good order, so as to maximise the possibilities of their lucrative trade. This one was clearly an exception. The boat, though the traditional long narrow shape, pointed at both ends with the standing step at the back, and the curved figurehead leading the way, was old and scruffy, the paint was peeling, and patches of oil had stained the interior. The smell of fish suggested it had recently been used to transport something other than wealthy lovers in search of the ultimate romantic experience, and as he shifted about in an effort to improve his view, Atticus realised his clothes were wet in places, so the boat was almost certainly not entirely watertight.

He pushed the tarpaulin further back and sat up. The tall buildings which had characterised the inner canal network had receded, and they were in a wider channel, passing bigger properties, set back from the water behind fences and gardens, most of them apparently uninhabited, their windows shuttered, security gates padlocked.

"Ees quite safe" said the gondolier, seeing Atticus. "They not come after you this far."

"Where are we going?" asked Atticus, although at this point he was rather past caring.

"We go to your 'otel of course," said the gondolier. "We go special way. 'Ow you say in Eenglish, the back passage," he sniggered.

"Right," said Atticus. "Well, Thank you. That will be...well fine. I think."

"You are musician, yes?" The gondolier whistled through a missing tooth, and indicated the cello case, which now had quite a nasty scratch across the lid.

"Yes," lied Atticus, thinking it was simpler.

"Is convenient no?" said the gondolier. "You 'ave big case, nobody guess you are carrying a dead man!" He laughed at his own joke. Atticus shivered.

Suddenly, the gondolier turned. "Queek!" he hissed. "You must go under the shit again. Police. They come."

Atticus heard the noise of a motorboat, and the gondola began rocking alarmingly. He ducked back under the tarpaulin, as the launch drew up alongside. Ropes were thrown back and forth to hold the two craft together, and someone heavy leant into the boat, sending water into the well where Atticus was hidden.

Expecting the conversation to be in Italian, he was surprised to find he understood it, before realising they were speaking English.

"Morning, Vince," said a gruff British voice. "You off somewhere interesting?"

"Good Morning Officer," said the gondolier, in what Atticus now noted was a decidedly patchy

Italian accent. "I am, 'ow you say, visiting my uncle."

"Your uncle is it?" said the officer. "I doubt that. In fact, I doubt that you have any relatives who would own up to you, let alone an uncle living out here. These palazzi cost millions."

"Yes," said Vince. "My uncle, he is very reech. He ask me to visit him. I expect he give me beeg present."

"Have you seen an Englishman, ordinary looking, medium height, medium build, possibly carrying a musical instrument?"

"I go to Philharmonic," said Vince, "I see many such men. Although not Engleesh. I only see Italian Philharmonic. I am Italian."

"Vince, everybody at the Stazione is well aware that you come from Huddersfield. In England" said the officer. "Have you or have you not seen this man, this afternoon?"

There was a pause while Vince was presumably being shown a picture.

"If I do," said Vince, "I shall arrest heem immediatemento. That jacket, he is a bad, crime."

There was another pause. "In fact he look familiar," Vince said. Atticus held his breath.

"Yes?" said the officer, "You know him?"

"No" said Vince. "E look like my cousin."

The officer banged a fist on the side of the boat. "You better not be up to something Vince" he said,

"Or I'll have you. I mean it!" He pushed the gondola off the side of the police launch.

"There's nothing here," he said to his colleague, "Come on, we're losing valuable time."

With a roar of the engine and another wide wash of canal water, the launch sped off.

Atticus put his head out from under the tarpaulin. Putting a hand out to steady himself, he realised it was covered in the slime he had felt on his face earlier.

"Thanks," he said, "Appreciate it. What exactly do you have under here?"

Vince snorted unattractively. "Ees Octopus," he said. "ees probably dead now."

Vince continued his erratic rowing, the boat making halting progress along the wide waterway, with Atticus sitting awkwardly in the bottom of the boat, feeling the fishy water seeping up through the seat of his trousers, scanning the canal on either side for any more unwelcome sailing companions.

"We gondolieri - we are not liking the police," Vince said. "They are on our case. They say we are not honest and they threaten to take away our licence. Then they ask for our help. Is not how you say in Eengland, cricket."

Atticus could now hear the decidedly Yorkshire twang in Vince's voice. "That octopus," he said, "did you catch it yourself? In the lagoon?"

"Of course," said Vince, sounding slightly shifty. "Is for my brother. He work in hotel. He has money for food to cook for guests. He will pay for this fish. But if anybody ask, you did not see any octopus."

"Fair enough," said Atticus. "You've done me a favour, I think I can be persuaded to keep quiet about our slippery friend."

Vince turned the gondola into a narrow channel only just wide enough for them to pass through,, struggling slightly as the boat scraped on the high walls on either side. The water was dark and oily, and the light was poor. Atticus began to wonder if he was ever going to get back to the Campanile Grande.

"You know Kate." said Vince. It was more of a statement than a question.

"Kate?" said Atticus, surprised, "Yes, yes I do. Is she a friend of yours?"

"Kate? She's a friend of everyone. She is magic."

"She does magic. Yes, I know I've seen her do it. Impressive. I need to find her. Do you know where she lives?"

"No. Kate does not tell me. She fancies me. But we are not yet lovers." Vince sounded pretty laid back about the inevitability of a relationship with Kate in the future. Atticus took another look at the filthy plimsolls, and the moth-eaten striped sweater, but he didn't get a chance to follow up Vince's confident assertion, because the gondolier was already tying the boat up to a rusty iron post which protruded from the wall. Beside the post was a heavy wooden door, which swung open when Vince hit it with the long oar he had been using to propel the boat.

"Is Vic," said Vince, as the door opened, and for a moment Atticus thought he was seeing double. A second man the image of Vince was standing in the doorway. "Is my brother, Victor." Vince explained. "We are twins. He works as porter here in your hotel. He will help us."

Vic, who was dressed in equally grimy clothes, but this time those of a kitchen porter, held out a hand and Atticus scrambled onto a small wooden step before being hauled in through the door. The cello was then handed up between the men.

"You can go through the kitchens," Vic said. Unlike his brother he made no pretence to the Italian accent. "Take the service stairs, you can get to your room that way."

"How do *you* know I'm staying here?" Atticus asked but Vic just raised an eyebrow. Any further conversation was cut short by the arrival of the octopus, which landed on the floor at their feet. Vince had untied the gondola and was already pushing off from the wall.

"Shit Man, what am I supposed to do with that? Vic said. "Where did he get it?

"He caught it," said Atticus, "In the lagoon."

"Right," said Vic, with another raise of the eyebrow. "Is that what he said? I'm surprised the Eyetie Fuzz aren't after him. He's nicked this from the Rialto fish market. Well anyway, it can't stay here. You'll have to help me hide it before chef sees it."

Atticus, already wet, weary, bruised and covered in a variety of identifiable and unidentifiable substances, sighed.

Chapter Thirty

As Atticus made his way up the back staircase of the hotel a few minutes later, still carrying the cello, he realised he had been so busy worrying about Laura, and the police, and Vince and the octopus, that he scarcely remembered the hotel. He hoped he was right in his vague memory of being on the third floor, and he hadn't worked out how he was going to get in. His room key had long been lost, probably stolen in the warehouse along with his watch and mobile. It would have been too much to imagine that Kate would have been able to retrieve that too, and anyway Kate wasn't here. Kate had probably run away, maybe even gone to the police. If she had witnessed the murder, she probably thought he had done it. Dear sweet, clever, funny Kate.

Downstairs in the foyer of the Campanile Grande, a visitor was ordering tea and trying not to baulk at the prices. Over twenty pounds sterling for a cup of tea, he said to himself, this had better be good. And he had better find Atticus soon, or he would be bankrupted before he had a chance to find out what was going on. He sat back in the immense silk upholstered chair and sent a text message.

Have reached hotel. Wish we were staying here, you'd love it. Although twins probably less welcome. Chairs are pale yellow. No sign of A yet, but will ask around. Love You. Hal.

Across the foyer, another Englishman, this one in a leather jacket and jeans, kept out of the way behind a huge ornamental tree. Every now and then he made a note in a little book he was pretending to read. His head was spinning because he'd had too much Italian coffee, in a small scruffy bar round the corner before he had got here. He was used to surveillance operations, but if you had to be hanging about for hours anywhere, this was a pretty swanky place to do it.

He was also keeping a careful eye on another character, a tall man with yellow-blonde hair, who had been sitting just inside the main doors for several hours without ordering anything or meeting anyone. The hotel reception was consistently busy, with guests checking in and out, luggage being loaded and unloaded from water taxis and vaporetti. Flowers and packages were directed and redirected, and a row of Italian women in very smart uniforms manned phones which seemed to be permanently ringing. It was, thought Graham, like a very small city, in the rush hour.

A waiter brought Hal's tea, and he was momentarily distracted by the vast tray, spread with silver pots of tea and water, and fine bone china. He was however, disappointed by the tiny, exquisite little wafer biscuit, in the shape of a bird which sat all alone on a wide plate. He was starving. Since leaving Heathrow that morning all he had eaten was a tiny chewy pastry on the plane, so anxious had he been to get to the hotel and start to try and find Atticus. It seemed odd to imagine his mild-mannered and unassuming brother-in-law here, in this grand place.

Hal, like many married men, was not as adept at people-watching as his wife was. He rather relied on Hilly to point out the interesting from the uninteresting, to notice clothes she liked and hated, to sort out who was related to whom and in what way, in any group, and to predict who would get up and storm out, where a couple were clearly having a row. Now he sat, busy with his tea, realising that he probably wouldn't know a villain from a member of the Royal family.

If he *was* going to spot a villain, he thought, he would choose that bloke with the dirty yellow hair by the door. He hadn't ordered any tea, hadn't met anyone, and hadn't brought anything to read. Hal immediately distrusted a man who hadn't brought anything to hide behind. He opened his own copy of *Le Figaro* and pretended to read. There was a picture on the front page, of a rather beautiful woman, taken with a long lens, apparently going to a party with George Clooney.

Then again, there was also that fellow in the leather jacket. He was definitely suspicious. For a start, he was clearly hiding behind that plant. And nobody over thirty wore a leather jacket these days. Especially indoors. Hal marvelled at the other beautiful people, in their lovely stylish clothes, women with perfectly styled hair, men in pristine knitwear and soft shoes, crossing the foyer. If tea cost twenty quid he couldn't imagine how anyone had enough money to stay here. Perhaps Atticus had been mistaken. Perhaps there was another altogether more ordinary hotel nearby, more like the slightly down-at-heel guest house Hal had booked, but with a similar name to the Campanile Grande. Campanile mildly-impressive. Campanile *Lite*. If so, Hal would never find him.

Upstairs, Atticus looked carefully both ways as he emerged from the staff stairwell on the third floor. The thick carpet stretched for miles in either direction, barely worn by the few select and expensively-shod feet which had trodden its pile since it had been laid. The corridor was quiet, all the matching doors closed. The maid service had obviously finished its turnarounds and towel replacements, and was yet to begin with the evening's bed turndowns and complimentary gift placement. Atticus was still only ninety percent sure that he knew which room was his, and that was only because he recognised the mirror on the wall opposite the door. Each time he had come out of his room, and seen himself in that mirror, with the backdrop of the room with its view out to the Grand Canal, he had marvelled at finding himself in such a place. There were other mirrors, matching ones at regular intervals along the corridor, interspersed with photographs of the many celebrity guests the hotel had welcomed, but his mirror had a particular mark on the artificially aged glass. He had noticed it straightaway, because it gave him a small spot, right in the middle of his forehead.

He edged his way along, passing more mirrors, and Marilyn Monroe and Brad Pitt and Matt Damon, on past Julia Roberts and someone he didn't recognise but might have been Ryan Gosling before he reached 'his' mirror. He stood, square on and looked at his reflection. This time the dot looked as though someone had shot him through the head with a very tiny bullet. He turned and looked at the door to his room.

He could wait for maid service and claim he had lost his key. He could wait for another guest and ask them to call down to the front desk for him. But both of these involved things he didn't want to do i.e. waiting, and drawing attention to himself.

He could put his shoulder to the door and hope it gave, or he could find a small implement and pick the lock. But he didn't believe he was strong enough to break the door down and anyway he didn't really want to add criminal damage to his already growing record of serious crime. And even if he knew what kind of a small implement one would need to pick a lock, and even if he knew how to do it, there was no lock to pick, the entry mechanism being entirely electronic. He needed a teenager with a laptop and a history of computer hacking.

He heard a noise at the far end of the corridor and instinctively tried to hide behind the cello. As if a man hiding behind a cello was any less suspicious than a man on the run without a cello. In desperation he put out a hand and tried the door handle. To his surprise, yet again, an apparently locked door swung open.

The first thing he saw was the chair with his pyjama trousers on it. Then he noticed his brown brogues, cast aside just twenty-four hours ago, when he had left this room in full evening dress, believing he was going to a nice party to meet interesting and influential people, with a beautiful woman on his arm. How everything had changed in those few hours.

He went in and closed the door behind him. Placing the cello carefully in the wardrobe, where a smarter guest would have put an overcoat or a full-length evening dress, he went to the window and reassured himself that everything at the front of the hotel was as it had been when he left. The canal was busy with its usual traffic of admiring tourists in vaporetti, and water taxis depositing and collecting hotel guests.

He took off the loathsome loafers and massaged his aching feet. Then he threw off the blue cashmere jacket and the once-crisp white shirt and left them in a heap on the floor. He suspected that he would never quite get around to asking the hotel staff to get them cleaned for him. He also suspected that pretty soon he would be leaving in handcuffs between at least two of the Venetian Statione's finest. However, in the meantime, what he was going to do, was have a bath.

He took off the rest of his clothes, and went into the bathroom to turn on the taps and choose a reviving bath oil from the extensive selection provided. He might at least meet his fate head on, properly dressed and clean.

And this time, two people screamed.

Chapter Thirty-One

"How was I supposed to know you were going to take all your clothes off before even checking the bathroom?" said Kate after a few minutes.

"How was I supposed to know there would be someone in my bathroom? How did you get in?" protested Atticus, aware of his naked reflection in the mirrors all round them.

"How do you think?" said Kate, "I'm a magician. It's on the starter course. Lesson One, or Two. I don't remember. Anyway at least I left the door open for you."

"How did you know I was coming?"

"Really? You have to ask? I thought you and Vince got on so well. He told me you did. He told me you were almost brothers."

"Did he?"

"He said he would allow me to wait here for you because he could trust you not to misbehave with me because *you* would know that I am promised to *him*, and you would never do that to your brother."

"And are you? promised to Vince?"

"What do you think? Come here you dear naked thing, and tell me exactly what happened outside Ziferelli's. Did you get to meet George Clooney?"

Atticus retrieved his dressing gown from the back of the door and wrapped himself in it. Kate turned on the taps in the bath and chose a purple bath oil.

"Very sexy," she pronounced sniffing it. "And the noise of the water will mask anything we say."

"You mean the room is bugged?"

"Might be. They think you did it you know."

"They think I killed Laura? But why would I do such a thing?"

Kate shrugged. "I don't think they're clear about motive. Yet. I expect they'll make one up while you languish in a Venetian prison. Anyway, it certainly seems there was rather more to the lovely Laura than met the eye."

"Yes, there was plenty which met the eye too."

"No need to rub my nose in it."

"I didn't mean...Oh, you know what I meant!"

"Luckily for you I do. God I'm starving. Is there any food in here?"

"In the bathroom? Unlikely."

"In this palace of a hotel room. Look, you get in and slosh about and I'll sort something out."

Atticus sank gratefully into the two-foot high foam which topped a further foot of the most delicious hot water he had ever encountered. As he drifted in and out of an indulgent doze, he thought he could hear voices, but he couldn't be sure. And when he emerged, as pink and fragrant as a baby, he saw a complete picnic laid out around his room.

Beautiful dainty sandwiches, small cakes, and little pieces of fruit were all arranged on tiered stands, with small mesh baskets of piping hot french fries and miniature burgers under small silver domes. Beside the bed was an ice bucket, filled with ice and his still unopened bottle of champagne.

"My God," he said, to Kate, who was standing in the middle of the room, wearing one of his shirts and precious little else, brandishing glasses and with a rose between her teeth. "You are some girl."

"I am not *some* girl," said Kate, turning down the bed. "I am *the* girl. Now shall we eat first or......?"

It was a tough call. But an hour later, as Graham, still wearing his leather jacket, opened the door to the room with a security pass, he found two people, fast asleep in each other's arms in the huge white bed, a plate of strawberries on the pillow and champagne still fizzing gently in the glasses. He took a turn round the room picking up items of useful evidence, made a note in his little book, and went downstairs to make a few calls.

"You know you've never told me anything about yourself," said Atticus happily, some hours later, as they nibbled on the last of the picnic, still wrapped in each other and the luxurious Egyptian 300-thread count duvet. "How did you come to be here, in this incredible city?"

"Ah," said Kate drowsily. "I've been here a long time. My parents brought me to Italy when I was eight. My Dad was a sound technician for films. He got a job on a Peter Greenaway film in Rome. Then, just when we were all settled and happy and learning to be Italian, it turned out he was also supporting another family, in Montesacro, one of the better suburbs, and as we lived one of the nastier suburbs, my Mum had a hissy fit and went back to England. I stayed with Dad and Sophia and my half-siblings, Paulo and Mastroianni for a bit, and as soon as I was old enough, I came here. The boys were always in trouble with the police. They taught me a lot, I can tell you."

Atticus saw bleakness in Kate's face, heard sadness in her words.

"Come here darling," he said, "You're safe now."

"Ah" said Kate, quietly "But am I?"

Atticus was asleep.

Chapter Thirty-Two

A few cobbled streets away, Hal awoke the following morning, feeling guilty for having had a deep untroubled sleep. The combination of worry over Hilly, years of sleep deprivation at the hands of the twins, and the joy of being in a large bed by himself had all combined, and after spending as long as he decently felt he could over the tea in the Campanile Grande, he had walked slowly back to his rather down-at-heel but pretty hotel, ordered a toasted sandwich and a beer, and gone straight to sleep.

He got up hastily, showered and dressed and headed back out into the City. He had to find Atticus and soon. If he was in trouble, it could be getting worse, and if he wasn't, Hal couldn't afford to stay here. Either way, he couldn't keep Hilly in suspense.

Meanwhile, Atticus had been awake since dawn. Gazing for a while at the sleeping Kate, he got up and paced the room for a while. He started by trying not to wake her, but when he tripped over one of the room service trays, sending silver and china crashing into each other with no response, he realised that Kate for one so small, was a very heavy sleeper. The eiderdown bag was slumped in a corner like a homeless person in a duvet curled up in a doorway, and he fought the impulse to look in it. Did he really want to know how the magic was done?

He opened the wardrobe intending to choose which of his two pairs of trousers he should put on. That was when he noticed that the sad remains of his dinner suit trousers, the pale blue jacket, the new shirt and the salmon sweater had all gone. Presumably room service had been in, he thought, only in a hotel as good as this would they remove dry cleaning without you even having to ask.

The cello was still standing in the wardrobe. Atticus ran a hand lovingly across its curves, trying not to mind the new scratches. Everybody started to show signs of the adventures they had sooner or later, he reminded himself. He got it out and stood it in the middle of the room.

He put on his jeans, savouring the joy of clean underwear and socks, and the twins' faintly biscuity handprint smell on his favourite sweater. As he went into the bathroom to clean his teeth and shave, he heard faint stirrings from the bed. Kate would wake up and see the cello. It would be a lovely surprise for her. She would be so pleased he had rescued it for her. Perhaps she would play it for him.

"Atticus?" Kate came into the bathroom behind him, so he could see her in the mirror. She looked marvellous, all messy and normal and sweet. He wondered briefly what Laura would have looked like first thing in the morning, and couldn't believe he had ever entertained thoughts of spending a night with anyone except Kate.

"What is that cello doing in the room?"

"Morning sweetheart. I knew you'd be pleased."

"Pleased? Why?"

"Because I found your cello for you!"

"My cello? It's not *my* cello."

Atticus turned. "What do you mean it's not yours?"

"I mean it's not mine. I don't own a cello. I don't even play the cello. In fact I don't play any musical instrument."

"Really?"

"Oh no, I forgot. Of *course* I'm a cello virtuoso. I'm the new Jacqueline du Pre, and this evening I'm due to deliver the Elgar *Cello Concerto* at Le Fenice with the Venetian Symphony Orchestra. I just forgot about it. *No* Atticus, like I said, I don't play the cello. I think I'd know if I did."

There was a long silence. Atticus washed his face and dried it on a towel.

"So if it isn't your cello, whose is it?"

"I've no idea. Where exactly did you get it, and why did you think it was mine?"

"Somebody gave it to me. At the restaurant. Where, where *it* happened."

"And did this someone not *ask* you if you wanted it, or if you knew whose it was? Why did he think you wanted it?"

"He said....." Atticus tried to remember. It had all become a bit of a blur. " I thought he said it belonged to you. Or maybe he said it belonged to a lady. I can't quite remember...."

Kate led him back into the bedroom. They sat on either side of the cello and looked at it.

"Right. Start at the beginning," she said, "When you first saw the cello."

Atticus wasn't sure he knew where to start. "It was at the airport," he began.

It was a long story, but Kate listened intently. He had to keep going back over the details as he remembered more and more, but as he spoke, he began to see that when he said it out loud, it was open to more than one interpretation. Kate didn't react however, even when he got to the bit about Boran and the crates. When he got to the bit on the bridge, she interrupted. "Oh yes, Vince" she said. "Well that was me. *I* told Vince to look out for you."

"Right. Thanks," said Atticus, confused.

"Well I had no idea where you would have gone."

"I thought *you* would think that *I* might have murdered Laura!"

"Oh no", said Kate "You wouldn't be capable of murder."

Atticus felt rather unreasonably insulted. "I daresay I could if I really wanted to," he said.

"No," said Kate, "You're just not the type. So if the cello isn't yours, and it isn't mine, and it has been pretty much wherever you've been, and is now here with us, and nobody has claimed it, how are we going to find out who owns it?"

"We could look inside," said Atticus.

"Open it?"

"Well I know that inside *my* cello case..."

"Wait! you *do* have a cello?"

"Well yes, at home. But I don't play it. At least I was having lessons. I thought I might..... look it isn't relevant, except that I put my name and address inside the lid of my cello case in case I lost it."

"Was that likely? In London? On your way to and from a cello lesson?"

"Well anyway, it just seemed sensible."

"Right" Kate stood up. "Well if you really want to open, it, go ahead"

"It's bound to be locked."

"Of course," said Kate. "So that's that then."

"Can't you open it? With one of your magic spells?"

"Magic isn't for opening locked things. That's just tricks."

Atticus went over to the window. As he looked down he thought he saw a familiar figure, getting out of a waterbus and heading towards the hotel. It couldn't be, surely. What would *Hal* be doing here?"

"Look," said Kate, "I'm starving, and we've eaten everything from last night. Let's go out. I know a great coffee bar not far from here."

"I can't go out," said Atticus. "I'll be seen."

"If they know where you're staying, it's only a matter of time before they come for you anyway."

"I know. I need to think. I suppose I should try and get a lawyer or something."

"Do you know any lawyers?"

"Funnily enough I do" Atticus thought longingly of Hilly. It must have been wishful thinking. He was so desperate to see a friendly face he had even imagined he saw Hal a few minutes ago.

"I don't have a phone remember? I don't want to go through the hotel switchboard."

"Use mine," Kate said, rummaging in the eiderdown bag. "Call whoever you want. I'm going to get some coffee. I'll bring you back Panettone. Then we can open the cello. Maybe you can play something for me." She handed him an iphone and kissed him on the top of the head. "Won't be long!"

Atticus sat, looking at the phone for a while. Whatever would he say to Hilly? That he had been so stupid as to think that a beautiful woman had wanted him to be with her? Hilly of all people would know what his track record was like. After Flora, she had even told him to stay away from women for a bit, to give himself time to recover and on no account to ever do such a dreadful thing to anyone again. She hadn't been exactly enthusiastic about Laura. And then, Oh God, yes, he had sent her a picture of Kate too. She must think he was on some womanising spree.

Laura had needed him, to keep her safe from the people she had got mixed up with, and he had failed her too. He was just a failure all round. How could he break the news that he had made another terrible mistake, and not only that, he was now on the run from the police, suspected of at least one and possibly two murders?

He looked at the cello case, still lying on the floor in the middle of the room. It was remarkably similar to his own. His had two lever clips on either side of its handle, and a single lock which sometimes jammed and could be worked open with a biro.

He sat on the floor next to it and ran his hands over the familiar shape. Levering the clips up, he wiggled the lock. It felt slightly loose. He reached for a complimentary biro from the hotel's stock of stationery on the ornate writing desk. Inserting the point into the lock, he twisted it about a bit. There was a click and the case opened with a sigh.

Atticus stared at what was inside.

"Well nobody is going to get much of a note out of *that*," he said aloud.

Lying in the cello case, filling its interior almost completely, was a black statue of a young naked man. Round his head were sculpted ribbons and he was holding a trident. The surface was smooth and lustrous. It was truly beautiful.

"Well that explains why the bloody thing's so heavy" he said to himself, "I'd bet that's bronze."

The realisation of what this new find might mean began to dawn on Atticus. If the statue was valuable, someone would be looking for it. If they found him with it, they would assume he had stolen it. On the other hand, if he went to the police with it, they might be grateful he had returned it, but they would almost certainly arrest him for the murders.

He got up and paced the room, turning Kate's phone over and over in his hand. He wished she would hurry up and come back so he could ask her what she thought he should do. Then he had an idea. Pressing the Google search button, he was reassured by the way it sprang into life, offering its usual gateway to the entire world. He was momentarily distracted by the possibility of Googling *Help I'm Wanted for a Murder I didn't Commit*, but instead, he typed *bronze boy with trident* into the search window.

A lot of heavy-looking text about Statues and Greek Gods came up and he scrolled through looking for something quick and easy to read. Halfway down the screen his eyes settled on a heading which read '*Greek statues stolen in Italian raid, recovered in New York*' and clicking on the link, a shiver ran down his spine.

There was a picture of a black bronze statue, which was uncannily similar to the one currently lying in its purple polyester satin-lined coffin in front of Atticus.

It seemed that a bronze statue, of the Greek God Zeus had been stolen from a museum in Rome in 1988, and had recently turned up in an art dealer's window in Manhattan. A keen-eyed Italian policeman on holiday had spotted it, and now it was being returned. The policeman had even been given a medal by a grateful nation. There was a picture of the statue, captioned '*Zeus, believed to be one of three 1st Century bronzes, estimated value £425k*' The other two it seemed, had yet to be recovered.

The statue in the picture was the recovered Zeus. The other two were Hades and Poseidon. Poseidon it appeared, could be recognised by his trident and the seaweed in his hair.

"Good God," said Atticus out loud, his eyes still on the mobile screen as he heard the door to the room opening. "Kate! You'll never believe this!"

The feeling of really expensive deep-pile carpet on his face was the last thing he remembered.

Chapter Thirty-Three

It was mid-afternoon when Atticus woke up again, still lying on the carpet,. He had a terrible headache, and when he staggered to his feet and made it to the bathroom he could see why. There was a large bruise on one side of his head, with dried blood setting in a nasty gash over one eye.

He poured himself a glass of water, savouring the warm brackishness of the water and only then remembering you weren't supposed to drink water out of bathroom taps in foreign countries, especially in countries where the water in question had probably been drawn straight out of a canal not a hundred feet away. Gradually he regained some memory from earlier. Where was Kate? She had gone out for breakfast, and never come back.

Then he remembered the phone, the last thing she had given him. Had he called anyone? Where was it now? And then he remembered the cello. Which was most definitely no longer in the room.

How many times was it possible to come to, after being unconscious in an empty room, and realise you'd been robbed? This was beginning to look almost like a habit.

Suddenly, Atticus had had enough. He would simply have to face the music if he was ever going to get out of this hotel, out of this city and out of the country. He picked up the Room Service phone.

"I want to go home," he said, when one of the bright young girls at Reception answered it. "I want to go home."

Within minutes, a square white envelope was pushed under the door. Picking it up he saw it was an itemised bill. Everything he had done since he arrived at the Campanile Grande was noted, from porters' gratuities, champagne, extensive room service, dry cleaning and shoe polishing. The figure at the bottom was a breathtaking total.

He checked the wardrobe, half expecting to find that someone had tidied the cello away, but instead seeing the dreadful pale blue jacket in a plastic wrapper, beside the salmon sweater, which was folded in tissue paper on a shelf. The shoes, sitting on a little mat underneath, looked almost as good as new, unfortunately.

There was no way he would be able to pay the bill. He might have been able to access it from his savings account, where Godfather Horatio's legacy was kept, and handed out carefully by an extremely old-fashioned bank, but he had no way of getting to it. He had no wallet, no credit cards, and no cash.

Atticus packed his few remaining belongings in the holdall, deciding against taking a selection of the bath products. He didn't want to be accused of anything else. As he tucked the salmon sweater in, he felt something hard and square in the bottom of the bag. Drawing it out, he realised it was the present he had bought for Laura. *Oh Lola*, by Marc Jacobs. The packaging still smelled of it, the scent hung heavy in the air, and he closed his eyes, seeing Laura standing there, in one of her silk evening dresses, her hair piled on top of her head, diamonds in her ears, and round her neck, her hand outstretched towards him. 'Come on Darling' she was saying, "Come with me, It'll be fun"

Suddenly he was just terribly tired. He lay back on the bed and closed his eyes.

"Signore?"

At the sound of Marco's voice, Atticus began to wake up. The light in the room had changed, as *l'ora d'or*, the golden hour of which tourists and Venetians were so enamoured, turned the last of the day into a pink-gold haze. That meant it was sometime between 6 and 7pm, and he had been asleep, either naturally or unnaturally, for the best part of the day. His head still hummed slightly, and for a moment he had no idea where he was.

Marco, in his pristine hotel uniform, stood over him.

"Signore Drake? You want I take your luggage to the taxi?"

Atticus sat up. "Taxi?" he said groggily.

"Si, Signore. Your friend, he say you need to be at airport for evening flight. You go now."

Friend. What friend? *He*, not *She*. There was no mention of the bill. Atticus, catching sight of it lying on the bedside table picked it up hastily and stuffed it into the back pocket of his trousers.

"Right. Right," he said. "Yes. The bag. It's all there I think. Nothing else. No hotel silver, no bathrobes." He laughed nervously. What *was* he gabbling on about?

Marco picked up the holdall. If he was surprised at its lightness, the fact that it was the sole article of luggage, or the fact that it smelt quite distinctly of a woman's perfume, he was too well trained to comment.

"We go," he said, indicating the open doorway into the hall.

Atticus put the powder blue jacket on. He thought it might be less obvious in this city of a million such jackets. He left the shoes.

As he left the room, Atticus turned. He had no idea what was ahead, but he wanted to take in, one last time, the view from that window. He was pretty sure he would never be in such a room again.

"'I'm sorry Laura," he said quietly, and shut the door.

As usual, the corridor was empty. Atticus began to wonder if there was in fact anyone else staying on this floor at all. He followed Marco to the lift feeling a mixture of guilt, because he didn't have a single cent on him to give the man as a tip, and apprehension. Surely the police would be waiting for him downstairs? Where was Kate? He needed to find her. She would tell them he was innocent, that he hadn't killed anyone, that he had accidentally got himself locked in a warehouse with a dead man, that Laura had been gunned down by someone else, coincidentally just in front of him, and that the apparently stolen statue had just been handed to him, that he had genuinely had no idea what was in the cello case. Kate was the answer.

The doors of the lift closed, and the two men stared ahead.

"My friend, the woman who was here with me last night?" Atticus said after a while.

"Signore?"

"My companion. She was here. She ordered room service? She went out this morning to get coffee. I wonder, do you know where she went?"

"For the coffee Signore? I do not know where she would go. There is excellent coffee here in hotel. I think you would order the coffee from your room."

"You didn't see her? My friend?"

"I see no-one Signore. You are in the room alone I think. Is sad in Venice, it is city of romance. You are on business maybe."

The lift reached the ground and the doors opened. Atticus waited.

Nothing happened. The lift opened out into the foyer, which emitted its usual expensive hum of rich people and discreet staff, going about their everyday business. Plants were being watered by a team of very sexy women in bright green monogrammed boiler suits. At the desk a bunch of huge men in long coats gave Atticus a moment's nervousness, until he saw that they were providing a surrounding cordon for a very tiny woman in a fur coat. It was the pop star he had shared the plane out here with. How strange, he thought, that she had been staying here too. The two of them had been just a few thin partition walls away the whole time.

Marco was waiting for him, holding the lift doors open. "Signore?"

"Yes," said Atticus. "Right." He scanned the room. There was nothing for it. When they got to the front desk, the bit where bills were settled, he would have to make a run for it. He calculated how he would grab his bag and which way he would go. He should turn right probably, past the display cases of ludicrously expensive jewellery, and out of the door at the end. That way he would come out onto a side street and not onto the long pontoon which ran the length of the front of the hotel. That way he wouldn't run the risk of falling into the canal in a chase, or worse, pushing someone else in.

Then he saw Yellowhair. He was sitting by the very door Atticus had earmarked for his escape. Yet again he was pretending to read. This time, it was celebrity people-watcher's favourite *Hello*. There was a picture of George Clooney on the cover, presumably at the very party Atticus hadn't been at. So the side door was out.

He continued to stand in the lift for a moment longer, before he realised that Marco had given up and gone on ahead. With his bag.

Perhaps they would let him phone Hilly from the front desk. But then what could she do? She didn't have almost three grand to hand over at a moment's notice. And besides, as soon as they realised he couldn't pay, surely they would call the police anyway. Who would be thrilled to find the murderer they were looking for, right under their noses.

If Atticus had phoned Hilly at that point, he would have found the number engaged.

"Where are you? Speak up, I can barely hear you!" Hilly, dragging a twin fastened securely round each knee round the room as she spoke, was exasperated.

"I'm trying to stay under the radar!" protested Hal, the phone held under the collar of his jacket. "I can't afford any more coffee in this hotel, and if they see me here again they're likely to throw me out as a vagrant."

"Don't be ridiculous. Just go to the front desk and tell them you're looking for Atticus! Either they'll have seen him or they won't."

"It's not quite as simple as that."

"What do you mean, it's not as simple as that? What's happening? Why won't you tell me?"

"The thing is, I don't think I'm the only person looking for him."

"Really? Who else would be looking for my little brother?"

"Just about everyone it seems. I've been here thirty six hours, and already I've seen three different people go to the front desk with what looks like a picture of said little brother."

"Oh God. I *knew* it! Something's happened to him!" Hilly was near tears.

"Hold on sweetheart, we don't know that. Maybe he's just gone out with one of what seems to be many possible girlfriends, and maybe these chaps are the girlfriend's boyfriends. Or husbands. Or fathers."

"Atticus would never do that! he would never mess about with a married woman!"

"This is Italy Hilly. To be honest, they seem to do things like marriage and father/daughter relationships rather differently here."

"Like the Mafia? Oh God, tell me the Mafia haven't got to him!"

"Don't be silly Darling, I'm sure it's nothing like that" Hal wasn't at all sure of any such thing, but he was acutely aware of the rising panic in Hilly's voice. "Look, I'm going to stay here a bit longer, and see if I can find out any more."

"But who are these people? The men who are looking for him?"

"Well...." Hal wondered how much to say to his wife. "There is a tall blonde man, possibly German..."

"German?!"

"Or maybe Austrian. You know, how I suggested that the second girl, the one Atticus sent the picture of might be German? Well I think he might be her father. Or brother. He's still here as it happens. He had a picture of Atticus at the desk yesterday."

"What business of his is it, who Atticus is going out with?"

"Quite. I expect he just wants to meet him. Ask him about his intentions towards the daughter, that kind of thing."

"Well that seems reasonable."

"Exactly. Then there was a scruffy chap in a leather jacket and jeans, yesterday afternoon. He had a picture too. He seems to have gone, although last night I'm sure I saw him lurking behind a pot plant. May have imagined it."

"Scruffy? In a place like that? That sounds suspicious. Does he look like a villain? Some kind of thug? Italian?"

"Not Italian. Not in those trainers. Do you know, all the men here have the most incredible shoes. Mind you they all look pretty smart. Lovely trousers. And they all seem so well turned out. Not like Brits."

"For God's sake Hal, I don't care about their bloody shoes! Why are they all looking for Atticus? Something's happened to him. I know it has."

"Try not to worry Darling. I'm going to stay here a bit longer, and see if I can find out anything more. He'll turn up. And if he doesn't show in the next couple of hours, I'm going back to the airport. My Easyjet ticket is non-transferable, so I'll have to come home anyway, and then we can decide what to do next."

"I wish I was there," said Hilly.

"So do I Darling, Venice is quite beautiful."

"Hal! I mean I wish I was there because then I could help you find Atticus."

"Oh quite. Well as I say, I'm sure there's nothing to worry about."

Hal ended the call with a smoochy kiss, which issued through the jacket collar sounded to Hilly a bit like someone being sick. He decided against telling her about the police who had already been into the hotel twice, brandishing their own pictures of someone who looked like Atticus but was wearing a very improbable jacket, so might not have been. Probably wasn't.

Atticus grabbed a copy of a magazine from a nearby table, and using it to shield his face, he walked carefully across the foyer, towards the front entrance of the hotel. His porter and his bag had already gone through the doors, and were presumably waiting for him outside, while he would be expected to pay his bill. He passed the front desk, appearing to be completely engrossed in a magazine article about cheesemaking in Parmigiano. For a moment he became genuinely engrossed, he liked a bit of Parmesan, and there were a lot of great pictures, despite the article being in Italian. Narrowly escaping a collision with a trolley laden with matching Louis Vuitton trunks, he made it to the doors and out into the sunshine. Then he stood and waited. Nothing happened. Nobody came. His porter was waving at the end of the jetty, and he saw a water taxi, bobbing up and down, its engine revving, ready for the off. Who had arranged the taxi?

Atticus shook Marco's hand, and got into the boat. He went down into the cabin and sat on one of the well-upholstered leather seats. The bill from the Campanile Grande cracked in his back pocket. The boat roared away from the jetty.

Inside the hotel, the blonde-possibly-German man tore a picture of Uma Therman out of the copy of *Hello* magazine and put it in his inside pocket. Then he got up and left the hotel. He liked Uma Therman.

Chapter Thirty-Four

The boat sped out into the lagoon, the thousand islands laid out like bits of a jigsaw puzzle. The wind got up, and Attics was torn between staying down inside the cabin, unseen and warm, and getting out onto the deck to fully appreciate the magnificent views. The City receded into the distance, shrouded in a light mist which made it look as though it was a mirage, and then as though it had never existed.

He went out into the air as the taxi passed Isola di San Michele, dark and foreboding, as silent as the thousands of graves it harboured. How would it be, he wondered, to be a Venetian, to know that you would end up there, ferried by a waterborne funeral procession and left in the dark, alongside centuries of noblemen and princesses, gods and rotters, sleeping amidst the ghosts of Venice past. He felt a chill run through his body but at the same time, he had never felt more alive. He wished Kate was with him, she was somebody who would completely understand. Of all the people he had ever met, Kate knew what it felt to be alive. She would love the idea of him leaving the Campanile Grande without paying a three thousand pound bill. He hoped she was alright. He felt bad about losing her phone.

"Everyone knows Kate." That's what Vince had said.

"Signore?" he said to the taxi operator, shouting over the roar of the diesel engine, "You speak English?"

"Si. Of course," the man shouted back, his eyes frowning in concentration, as he steered the boat across some choppy side currents.

"I wondered if you might know a friend of mine."

"A friend of yours Signore ? Why would I know him. You are a tourist!"

"Well yes. In a way. But my friend, well she lives here."

"She is Venetian?"

"Well no, but..."

"Not Venetian, I not know her."

Atticus remembered something he had once read about Venetians. That they are Venetian first, Italian second.

"I just thought you might. Her name is Kate. Pretty girl, does magic tricks, in the streets."

Atticus thought he saw a flicker of something cross the man's face.

"You do know her?"

The look was gone. The man shook his head. "I have not good English. I not understand you English accent."

Atticus gave up and went back inside the cabin for the remainder of the journey. As the boat neared the jetty he saw the queues of airline passengers who had just been unloaded from incoming flights, standing in lines, anxious to get moving and into the City of their dreams. Just a few short days ago, that had been him, he thought. A man on a fabulous holiday, not a care in the world other than whether he would enjoy a swanky party with a beautiful woman. And now, as the taxi operator threw the rope to a handyman on the dock and killed the engines, Atticus's foremost thought was whether he would get through the crowd and into the airport, and ultimately into the air and away before being arrested for a double murder and the smuggling of stolen art treasures.

Luckily the crowd massed towards him as he stepped ashore, his holdall gripped tightly to him. He turned to start the inevitable row over payment for the trip but the driver was already handing another fare into the cabin.

"I...er...I'm sorry, the thing is...I'll have to give you my address in the UK," Atticus shouted, embarrassed at conducting the conversation in front of an overheated family with three children.

"Do you mind?" the woman said, indicating her many cases.

Atticus put his bag down and started loading the family's luggage onto the boat.

"Not like that!" shrieked the woman, "That's Mulberry!"

"Signore?" Atticus shouted at the driver. "About the fare!"

""Is paid," shouted the driver, "Your friend. 'E pay already."

My friend again, thought Atticus. "What did he look like? My friend?" he shouted.

But the driver was already throwing the ropes back into the boat, and revving up the engine. Mrs Mulberry was thrown backwards onto a pile of her children as they sped off.

Atticus picked up his own bag and followed the signs into the airport. There were plenty of security guards and policemen about, all carrying an alarming amount of military-style hardware, but by carefully surrounding himself with other people, and freight trolleys, he managed to get inside the terminal building without attracting any attention.

He found the ticket and his passport in the outside zipped pocket of his bag, tucked inside the unopened copy of Hemingway's masterpiece. He was immediately thankful he had left them there and not in his stolen wallet. The smell of *Oh Lola* clouded the air again, and his heart bounced, just once more. Could he actually risk checking in his bag? With carry-on luggage only he would skip at least one dangerous stage, but he would still have to go through security and the scanner system.

He looked up at the departure boards, and found the right gate number. He had plenty of time, and as he sidled carefully towards the scanning queue, he allowed himself the luxury of looking in the windows of the smart shops, where smarter travellers than he were scooping up Duty Free bargains and spending their last few Euros on things they didn't really want.

And then he saw him. Yellowhair. He was in a luxury leather shop, trying on shoes. Every now and then he would walk up and down, admiring himself in the mirror, and somehow, his very existence suddenly seemed to represent everything Atticus had gone through. It was too much to believe that his permanent presence within a few yards of Atticus had been anything other than intentional. And if he was following Atticus, he must know everything that had happened. That Atticus hadn't killed anyone. And yet he had done nothing to help.

Unforgivable.

Atticus strode into the shop. Dropping his bag loudly on the floor, right beside the socked feet of his stalker, he looked up, and up, noticing first how tall the man was when up close.

"You," he said, sounding braver than he felt. "I want a word with you."

The man said nothing.

"I've just about had enough of you," Atticus said even more loudly. "You've been following me ever since I arrived. I want to know just what you think you're doing."

The shop assistant emerged from the stockroom carrying a pile of shoeboxes. Seeing a potential altercation, he backed back behind the counter, dropping the boxes and taking the chance to duck behind the counter after them.

"Well?" shouted Atticus, "What have you got to say for yourself?"

The man looked Atticus up and down.

"I want to know why you're following me."

Suddenly the man grabbed Atticus by the arm. "Shut *up*" he hissed.

Attics saw red. Swinging his free arm he took a punch and made contact with Yellowhair's square heavy-set jaw. Surprised, Yellowhair skewed sideways, and lost his balance, his feet without shoes slipping on the polished floor. He used his own free arm to steady himself, grabbing Atticus's jacket. The momentum was not enough to hold him upright, and both men fell to the floor.

Suddenly, the two men became three, as a third man, in a waxed cotton jacket and fading corduroys ran into the shop and launched himself at both men.

"Enough!" the third man roared, trying to pull Yellowhair off Atticus. The surprise was enough for both men to look up, and Atticus was startled to recognise this third member of the middle-aged men's fight club.

"Hal? Whatever are you doing here?" he asked. Yellowhair sat up, rubbing his chin where Atticus had despite the odds, managed to deliver a slight graze. The assistant reappeared with another box of shoes.

"More importantly, what the *hell* are you doing?" Hal said. "Starting fights in posh shops, whatever next? And what are you wearing? You look like a Holiday Camp rep!"

"This man," spluttered Atticus, "Has been following me ever since I arrived."

"Is that right?" Hal asked Yellowhair, "Do we know you? Wait a minute.... We *do* know you! You were in the hotel yesterday. And this morning. I *saw* you!"

Yellowhair fished in the pocket of his jacket, while trying to straighten his collar. He scrambled to his feet. He handed Hal a small plastic wallet.

"Blimey" said Hal, looking at it.

"What?" said Atticus, with a sinking feeling. "What does it say?"

"It says Interpol," said Hal. "This chap's an international copper. And you've just landed a punch and wrestled him to the floor. In his socks."

"Oh, *great*." said Atticus. "Why didn't you say something?" he said to Yellowhair. "What's your name? And that still doesn't explain why you've been following me."

"His name is Willem KugelNager," said Hal, reading the card.

"Sorry," said Atticus to Willem, who was still nursing the place where Atticus had hit him.

"Is OK," said KugelNager, "Is not so bad."

"I mean, I'm sorry about the KugelNager thing. That's a hell of a name to live with."

"And it doesn't sound Italian." Hal pointed out.

"German," said Willem. "I'm German. From Frankfurt. I"m on special detail here."

"German! What's a German policeman doing in Venice?" said Hal.

"Hardly the point," said Atticus "The fact remains, I seem to have been followed by the police even before I did anything wrong!"

"Before? What do you mean 'before'? You mean you *have* done something wrong now? Oh God, don't say you've got into some mess over a woman."

Atticus looked at his brother-in-law.

"Of course I haven't."

"Well that's a relief."

"No, not over a woman. It's much worse than that."

Willem KugelNager seemed disinclined to say anything more. Instead, he put his shoes back on, nodded his thanks to the assistant, who was furious at having missed out on what he had judged to be a certain sale, and went outside. where he proceeded to make a long and intense call on his mobile.

Chapter Thirty-Five

"Murder?" Hal was incredulous.

The two men sat at one of the airport's many coffee bars, perched like little birds on impossibly high stools, while baristas in brown jackets dispensed espressos and cappuccinos with lightning speeds, and anxious and tired travellers shuffled from foot to foot, knocking back the thick black brews with equal speed. At a table nearby, Willem KugelNager continued to make calls.

"I know. I couldn't believe it. At least KugelNager knows I didn't do it. Now I'm more interested in following *him*. He may be the only one who can get me out of this."

"But why you? And how did *you* end up with the cello?"

"I can't imagine. I can only think that Laura got herself mixed up in something by accident, maybe with that Boran. He looked like a bad lot from the start, and she was probably hoping I might rescue her in some way."

"You?"

"Why not me?" Atticus was affronted. Why did nobody believe he was capable of a heroic gesture, should the mood take him? "I was a reliable sort at school, and I competed in the Under-11 fencing championships. She probably remembered that."

"*Or*" said Hal, "You know, there is another possibility?"

"Really?" said Atticus, "Oh, I see. You mean that Laura didn't know she was mixed up in crime. Yes, yes I suppose that is possible. Poor Laura."

"That wasn't quite what I was thinking. And what about this Kate? You say she just left you to get mugged in your own hotel room?"

"Well she didn't know I was going to get mugged did she? No, I suspect she went out for the coffee, and got waylaid, or maybe she had a job to pull together the money for a bun or something. At least I hope that's what happened. I don't like to think she might have been targeted by these mobsters too. She'll never forgive me. Unless...."

"Yes?"

"I can't bear to think of it."

"Of what?"

"That they might have....Kate. Like Laura, they might have... Oh, and it's all because of me."

Hal said nothing.

"But you still haven't explained why *you're* here!" Atticus pointed out.

"Ah" said Hal. "Well the thing is..."

Around them, the life of the airport went on.

"I *know* Graham" said Atticus at one point. "Hilly worked with him on a couple of quite high profile cases, just after she qualified. He's OK, and I'm pretty sure he fancied her, but that was years ago, and he really isn't her type. Anyway, she would never do that to you!"

"She went to see him, without telling me, and she phoned him several times," Hal confessed. "I just lost my head over it. I know you're right. I just don't know what I'd do without her."

"You won't have to do anything without her. My silly old sister's lucky to have you." said Atticus reassuringly.

"So what does Graham look like, anyway?" Hal asked.

"Can't really remember," said Atticus. "Biggish build, but not particularly tall. Lots of hair, curly. Scruffy, but then he's a plain clothes policeman, and they always wear terrible clothes. They spend years wearing uniform and eating doughnuts, and then when they make it to CID they just put on the same stuff they used to wear, never mind that it's decades out of date and doesn't fit any more."

"Well you're clearly the sartorial expert," said Hal drily, indicating the powder blue jacket.

"Quite. Well I've explained that" said Atticus huffily. "Although I remember now, Graham wore a leather jacket everywhere. I quite envied it at first, in the Seventies. I don't think I ever saw him without it."

"Like an aviator jacket? With a biggish collar?"

"That's it. Quite unusual."

"Like *that* aviator jacket?" said Hal, looking past Atticus's shoulder.

Atticus turned and looked. "*Exactly* like that one" he said.

Graham walked straight past Atticus and Hal and over to Willem, who stood up and shook him warmly by the hand. The two of them had a short exchange of words, looking all round as they did so, and Willem indicated Atticus with a faint nod.

Graham came over. "Good God mate, I would never have recognised you!" he said to Atticus, "You used to be a tweed and cords sort of man." He looked at the blue jacket. "Well, well, Hilly's little brother! You've led us all a right old dance haven't you?"

"Hello Graham," said Atticus, not terribly taken with this greeting. "I wouldn't put it quite like that."

"I would." said Graham. "We've had half of Europe out after you. Who's this?"

"I'm Hal," said Hal slightly too loudly, "I'm...."

"Hilly's husband," said Graham, slightly less enthusiastically. "And what are *you* doing here?"

"I came to look for Atticus," said Hal quietly.

"You too eh? Hilly didn't tell me."

"Well I hardly think she would tell you *everything,*" said Hal, "And at least *I* managed to find him."

"You did mate, you did" agreed Graham, pulling up a chair and sitting down. "Well here we are." He turned to Atticus. "You got the taxi alright? No trouble at the hotel?"

"It was you," said Atticus "*You* paid the bill. And the taxi fare."

"Well we had to get you out. Expensive though. Not many of our witnesses get five star treatment."

"Witnesses?" said Hal and Atticus together.

"Well you are a witness, aren't you?" We've been on this case for eighteen months, and just as we're looking at a dead end, in you come, blow the whole thing open, and we get to start over again. We're very grateful, don't get me wrong, but you did order some mighty pricy room service, and you could have got yourself killed."

"I didn't exactly do it on purpose," said Atticus. "The being almost killed bit. The room service was pretty much on purpose."

"Well you'll be alright now. But I'm afraid we haven't quite finished with you."

Chapter Thirty-Six

"I can't believe this," said Atticus a few moments later. "You want me to stand in the middle of a busy airport, and pretend to be getting on a plane, - but not *actually* get on a plane -because you believe that whoever murdered Boran and Laura is going to have a go at me, because he believes I'll tell you who he is and about the stolen Poseidon?"

"That's about it," said Graham. Willem nodded enthusiastically, his yellow curls bobbing up and down.

"Even though 'having a go at me' might well involve actually killing me."

"Well obviously it won't come to that," said Graham. "We've got men all over the airport. They'll be on him before he has a chance to shoot."

"You think shooting will be the favoured method of taking me out?"

"Well from what you've told us, Boran was stabbed, but Laura was shot. That tells us that when the killer has time, he gets close to his victim, but when he's under pressure, he chooses to work from a greater distance. My money's on a shooter."

"Great. Well as long as we've got that sorted out," said Atticus." I'd hate you to lose a bet."

"I'm not sure this is a good idea," said Hal. "What if the killer succeeds? It's too big a risk. Can't you use, someone from your lot, a decoy?"

"We haven't time to set it up," Graham said, shaking his head, "If he suspects for a minute we're onto him, he'll slip away in this crowd and we'll be back to square one. He might even get the statue onto a plane."

"I hardly think the statue is the most important consideration here," said Hal.

"It's worth about five hundred thousand," said Graham.

"Well...even so," said Hal, sounding a bit less certain.

"I'll do it," said Atticus.

"Really?" said Hal.

"Great," said Graham.

They all looked at Willem, who looked bemused for a moment and then gave a thumbs-up sign.

"What do I have to do?" said Atticus.

"How the hell will I tell Hilly?" said Hal.

"You can't tell Hilly!" said Graham and Atticus together.

"Go with Willem," said Graham, "He'll fix you up with some kit, a stab vest and a wiretap so we can hear what's going on."

"A stab vest? I thought you said I won't be stabbed."

"Well, absolutely. But we might as well cover all eventualities."

Willem stood up and indicated that Atticus should follow him. Hal and Graham sat in silence for a bit.

"So," said Graham eventually, "You're Hilly's husband."

"Yup," said Hal.

"I've heard a bit about you."

"Have you?"

"I love her you know."

"Really. She never mentioned that to me."

"She wouldn't. She doesn't really know. And for the record, I am 100% sure that she doesn't feel the same way about me."

"Right. Well that's got that sorted out."

"Not really. Not for me. For me it sucks."

"No. I can see that."

"Anyway, just so as you know."

"Yeah. Thanks. Well maybe...you should come round sometime. Have supper with us. The twins'll probably put you off marriage and children for life anyway."

"I doubt it. But thanks anyway."

The two men sat in silence a little longer, before the slight but spreading thaw between them was interrupted by the sight of Atticus, carrying a much larger holdall than the one he had arrived with, and with the blue jacket bulging at its spare Italian-designer seams, walked across the concourse, pretending to study the departure boards.

"Right, that's me on duty," said Graham, leaving the table.

"What do you need me to do?" said Hal, but Graham had gone.

Hal got as close as he could to Atticus, and leant nonchalantly against a pillar, where he was regarded with interest by a small boy, carrying a stuffed aardvark.

Chapter Thirty-Seven

Atticus was sure that whoever was listening to his wiretap would be able to hear nothing but the thump-thump of his heart. It was a very odd feeling, being alone in a sea of people, knowing that you could be the target of a lethal attack. One minute you were alive and well, if with slightly raised blood pressure, the next you could be dead. Completely dead. He wondered if his life should be flashing before his eyes, but it wasn't. The only thing flashing before his eyes was the departure board, where planes were announced, filled, and took off, full of people being lifted high up in the sky and spirited away to exotic destinations, Marrakech, Oslo, St Petersburg, Aberdeen.

If his life *wasn't* flashing before his eyes, perhaps he wasn't dying. But who decided?

Inexplicably, he felt sad. Either way, he was just moments away from the end of this adventure, a reluctant participant in a real-life drama, and the centre of an elaborate but very important international business. And when those same moments were up, it would all be over, and, assuming he was still alive, he would go back to being Atticus, nice but basically unimportant guy, no proper job, no wife, no children, and no real idea about what he was actually put on Earth *for*.

Then again, he had been spared. Boran and Laura and goodness how many before them had not. Perhaps that in itself was a message. Perhaps that in itself was the reason. That he should be left alive at the end of this, was a message to him to do something. To make a difference. That was it. That was what he would do. He would do *something*.

Suddenly his train of thought was interrupted by a familiar voice.

"Tix? Tix? It *is* you! Oh Thank God. I was so worried. I thought I'd lost you! I thought they'd got you! That I would never see you again, and you would be thrown in some dreadful prison and probably extradited or exiled or excommunicated!"

Atticus turned and the first thing he saw was Kate, all auburn curls and eiderdown bag and wearing another of her fantastic embroidered coats, enveloping her in peacock tails and gold thread. He threw out his arms to greet her, and that was when he saw the second thing.

Her other hand was resting on the cello case.

Committed to the forward movement, but not at all sure he wanted to continue, he tripped, and fell into Kate's arms. He felt her hug him, a lovely, floral fragrant female embrace, but then, with something altogether different in it, a sort of hard, steel, delivered right into his side.

He fell back, unable to work out what had happened. The airport concourse spun round and round, leaving searing horizontal yellow departure-board lines in the air round his head. Men were shouting, running. Then the noise went away, and everything began to go dark. A small boy ran across the floor and looked down at him. Atticus looked up into five year-old eyes.

"D'you want to hold my aardvark?" the boy asked, and Atticus was surprised to find he couldn't think of the answer.

Chapter Thirty-Eight

The 18.30 Marco Polo to London Heathrow took off on time. In the 60 rows of Economy Class, tired holidaymakers, jaded honeymooners, and anxious businesspeople settled down for the trip, and prepared themselves fro the rest of their lives, which would begin just as the plane landed.

In the First Class section, two burly uniformed policeman sat, squeezed into their seats, with a red-haired woman in a peacock coat scowling and writhing, handcuffed between them. In front of them, several more members of several police forces in various bad suits, filled out paperwork, updated their statements, and worked up their expenses.

In front of *them*, Hal and Graham, drained and weary, sat on either side of the central aisle, which was occupied by a hospital trolley, on which Atticus, wrapped in blankets and with a drip in his arm, lay.

"I'm fine. Really," Atticus said at intervals. A private nurse shushed him and fiddled with the drip.

"It's nothing." he protested.

"You should have prevented this," said Hal to Graham.

"I know. But at least we had the stab vest."

"How did it happen? You said it wasn't possible."

"We were looking for a man."

"It is hard to believe. She looks so small. And nice."

"Well she maybe small but she certainly isn't nice. She's been eluding us for years. Ever since the late eighties. Statues, paintings, gold, jewellery. She's done it all. The stupid thing is, she's on the files of every force from Birmingham to Bosnia. She's been done for shoplifting so many times nobody can really be bothered to fill out the paperwork. That's what did it really. It was the best disguise she could possibly have given herself. Getting arrested every now and then for mobiles and watches, meant we would never in a million years have suspected she was at the centre of an international smuggling ring. Now she's confessed, it turns out the whole story is a lot bigger, and darker than even we suspected."

"How many of them are there?"

"Well we knew about Boran Bouboul. We'd been following him for quite a while. He was pretty near the top. We believe she axed him because he failed to find a courier for the Poseidon. He knew too much but he couldn't deliver. He was trying to recruit someone, which is probably where Laura Hutchinson fits in. She would probably have been too high profile to do the job herself, but that's where...." They both looked at Atticus.

"That's where I came in right?" he said sadly.

"Seems Hutchinson lost her nerve about recruiting him though. Boulboul must have told Miss Big here, who arranged for him to be kidnapped and drugged, keep him out of the way until they decided what to do with him. When Boulboul was killed, Hutchinson must have thought she'd got away with it. Anyway we think she told Kate here she wasn't going through with it, and that's when she signed her own death warrant."

"So what was I supposed to do?" said Atticus

"You were supposed to carry the cello home to England. Once the cello was in your house, there'd be a neat burglary, nothing out of the ordinary, and hey ho, cello is in the UK where there is a buyer. Anyway as soon as you opened the case and saw Poseidon, the game was up."

An in-flight announcement told them they were halfway home. A stewardess brought tea and some biscuits. Hal looked at the plate.

"That's one thing I won't miss about Italy," he said, "These pathetic little biscuits."

"With you there," said Graham "Give me a Hobnob any day."

By the time they landed, Atticus felt well enough to sit up and dispense with the trolley, in favour of a wheelchair. His whole body ached, and his chest strained against the tight bandaging which pressed against the small but deep wound he had sustained, just between the straps of the stab vest. He wondered if Kate had stabbed anyone else wearing protective gear in the past. She had certainly known where to strike. Maybe it was just luck. As he was helped gingerly down the steps and into the chair, with Hal and Graham on either side, he saw Kate being escorted off at the back of the plane. It was inevitable that the two parties would meet at the entrance to the terminal building.

"Why didn't you kill me when you had a chance?" Atticus said to Kate, as she regarded him with her deep eyes, now angry and free of the light he had so loved.

"I was aiming for you," she said, "When I shot Laura. I didn't mean to kill her. I quite liked her. She was supposed to carry the statue. It really annoyed me when she brought you along.   I couldn't work out why she'd done that. So I was aiming for you. I just missed."

Kate was hauled off to a waiting police van, the cello loaded carefully into the boot of another car. Atticus remembered his departure, just a few days ago, when he had seen sinister people in limousines on the tarmac. Now he was one of them. Funny how things turned out.

As Atticus was wheeled through the Nothing to Declare channel, he regretted not bringing some of the hotel bath products with him. Almost immediately, he was greeted by a crowd of squeaking wriggling people, arms and legs flailing, scrambling up onto the wheelchair, and which turned out to be the twins. Behind them, scolding and trying to protect the medical equipment still attached to him, was Hilly, half laughing, half crying.

"You stupid man" she said through tears.

"Sorry Hils," said Hal, Atticus and Graham all at once.

EPILOGUE

"Nobody will ever believe you" Hilly said, as they settled into her cosy sitting room, ignoring the thump of twins playing Horse of the Year show in the nursery overhead. Hal busied himself in the cluttered kitchen, making supper, and Hilly, after a futile attempt at reminding Atticus that he was on all sorts of painkillers, poured huge glasses of red wine. Atticus breathed in the marvellous, safe, family atmosphere, savouring the piles of papers and books, the small heaps of toys and half-eaten fishfingers.

"Why won't they believe me?" said Atticus. "What is it about me? You all seem so sure that I couldn't ever do anything interesting, or brave or important."

"Don't be silly," said Hilly. "You're very interesting *and* brave *and* important."

"Thank you," said Atticus, mollified.

"Just not in that way."

"Right."

"Spaghetti Carbonara alright with everyone?" called Hal from the kitchen. "Ees Italian!"

THE END

Atticus Drake will be back soon in: *The Funeral of the Sardine*. In the meantime, why not check out <u>www.torabarry.co.uk</u> for news of upcoming publications, promotions, and the writer's blog.

ACKNOWLEDGMENTS

My thanks to the following people, who made the writing and more importantly the finishing, of this book possible: To Chris Howard for the cover design, the first time I believed it was a 'real' book, to Nick Hindley, the Fromester, who has rescued me, and the manuscript from the unfathomable recesses of Apple Mac, and to Martin Phillips who provided the stability and confidence I needed to do it. Thanks to Celina Grace, writer of the marvellous Kate Redman mysteries, who generously gave me her time, as well as her tips and hints for publishing, and to Katherine Fenton, for her kind and skilful eye when it came to editing.

Thanks to friends and supporters who issued rallying cries, buns and drinks in equal measure, in particular but not exclusively, Jo (the mother of princes) Fulton, Caryl (Ezza) Hodgson, Alexis (The Dancing Trousers) Thompson, my favourite newly-weds Mrs Young and Mrs Spring-Rice, my extraordinary sister Lucy, and as ever and always, JKEH.

GOING GOING GONDOLA

TORA BARRY